The Cradle

ALSO BY PATRICK SOMERVILLE

Trouble: Stories

The Cradle
A Novel

PATRICK SOMERVILLE

Little, Brown and Company

New York   Boston   London

Little, Brown and Company
Hachette Book Group
237 Park Avenue, New York, NY 10017
Visit our Web site at www.HachetteBookGroup.com

First Edition: March 2009

Little, Brown and Company is a division of Hachette Book Group, Inc. The Little, Brown name and logo are trademarks of Hachette Book Group, Inc.

The characters and events in this book are fictitious. Any similarity to real persons, living or dead, is coincidental and not intended by the author.

Library of Congress Cataloging-in-Publication Data
Somerville, Patrick.
   The cradle : a novel / Patrick Somerville. — 1st ed.
      p. cm.
   ISBN 978-0-316-03612-2
   I. Title.
   PS3619.O45C73 2009
   813'.6 — dc22   2008025148

10   9   8   7   6   5   4   3   2   1

RRD-IN

Printed in the United States of America

I

Out of the cradle endlessly rocking,
Out of the mocking-bird's throat, the musical shuttle,
Out of the Ninth-month midnight,
Over the sterile sands, and the fields beyond, where the child,
*   leaving his bed, wander'd alone*

— WALT WHITMAN

1

Marissa could not be comforted, and wouldn't have it any other way. The cradle for the coming baby had to be the cradle she'd been rocked in as a child; not only the cradle she'd been rocked in but the cradle that was upstairs in her bedroom when she was fifteen and her mother came home one night from the grocery store, slammed her keys down on the countertop, slammed the brown crinkled bag onto the table, looked down at the floor, looked at Marissa, took the keys, and walked out the door, this time permanently. Ten days later there'd been a robbery at the house. Wouldn't you know it, many of Mrs. Caroline Francis's favorite things had been stolen and not very many of anyone else's favorite things had been stolen, so Marissa and her father had always assumed the robbery had been Mrs. Caroline Francis's transparent version of getting what she wanted for the start of her new life without having to walk in and see anyone or do a painful thing like say good-bye. The cradle was taken that night.

They said the cradle came from the Civil War. Matt had never believed that, no matter how many times he'd heard the story. What poor family living outside Milwaukee had Civil War relics in their home, and furthermore, who used such things, if they even existed, for actual children? Also, what exactly did a Civil War cradle look like? Did it have guns on it? Were there Confederate and Union flags carved into the headboard? What antique dealer had ever confirmed its origin? Had it been to Gettysburg? And whose baby was in it back then? Ulysses S. Grant's? Or the child of some Wisconsin soldier from the prairie who'd gone south to fight and never come back? There was no story attached to it and no good reason why the Francis family should have been so caught up with it.

But they were, and Marissa wouldn't have it any other way. She told this to him eight months into her pregnancy, her belly taut and round like a globe. It was June 1997, hot, and Matt was killing himself at work. He'd been taking whatever double shifts anyone at the plant dangled in front of him just to store up enough money for the baby. He had no idea what it meant for the kid to come and no idea what it was going to feel like once it came, so the one thing it made sense for him to do, he figured, was put his head down and get money in the bank and leave the understanding to Marissa or her father, two people who seemed to know quite a lot on the subject.

They were drinking lemonade on the back porch when she told him that the baby would be requiring the cradle.

She said it with her hand on the glass, staring at Matt straight in the eyes.

He said, "Well, how am I supposed to get it?"

"It's not like she broke it up into firewood. She's still got it."

"That doesn't matter much if we don't know where she is," he said.

"I think you'll be able to find her," she said. "I don't want to find her. I don't want to see her. I don't want to know how you do it or where she is. But you can, if you look hard enough. You can find anything. You're Matt. What about my keys? I look for six hours, then you get home and you find them in five minutes." Marissa aimed her dark countenance at him and waited. Her eyes were a deep chocolate black, like her hair, back now in a loose ponytail. She had a little birthmark that hugged her right nostril, and freckles up beneath her eyes. In the last month or so her skin had taken on a new tone — not exactly a new color, but rather a new timbre, infused with a ruddier health and light. She was not smiling.

"That's not the same thing. I'm sorry."

"I just want you to get it and bring it back."

Matt kept looking at her face. He was pleased to go to the grocery store to get her pickles in the middle of the night. He did suspect she was making it up half the time, of course, that half the time she wasn't really feeling any food cravings but was just acting out something about pregnant women she'd seen on TV. But he rolled out of bed and did it every time and never said one word. Fine. Going off to find her mother or an ancient cradle was different.

He looked up at Glen, his father-in-law, who was manning the grill about fifteen feet away and who was too deaf to overhear the conversation. "What will your father think?" he asked.

"I haven't said anything to him," said Marissa. "I don't know what he'll think. Maybe you should say something. He might have things he wants you to get back, too."

5

"Baby," he said, shaking his head at her grin, "I can't tell if you're joking right now or not."

"Just because I'm laughing doesn't mean I'm joking," she said. "That's rarely the case. You know me, Matt. The baby needs it."

"Why?"

"Because it matters, that's why," said Marissa. "Because every time I think about him in the world, I think about him inside of it. I don't want him growing up in some white plastic piece of trash that we order out of a catalog. That came halfway around the world. What lesson do you think we would be teaching by doing that? *I* was in that cradle, Matt."

"That's it," Matt said. "No one else. It's not as though your family's had the thing since the damned Civil War. Your grandma bought it at a yard sale."

"Right there, then. There's another link. Her hauling it home that day. Where it first came from doesn't matter. It's what it's done since then. I want it back. You of all people should understand this."

"Why?"

"You're an orphan." To her, the whole truth of the connection was obvious.

"How exactly does this relate?" Matt said, because it wasn't to him.

"There are two kinds of people in the world," Marissa said. "There are people who understand that everything matters and people who don't understand that everything matters."

How Marissa it was to say that. Matt smiled at her halfheartedly, leaned back into his chair. She was keen on breaking the world into its parts; she wanted its pieces on the table in front of her. Matt didn't know where this habit came from, this analytic aspect of her world. It certainly wasn't her father's way. Her father was all gray and compromise. Maybe Caroline had that to her. Or maybe it happened to you when you had a mother and then suddenly did not. Your mind, shifting miracle that it was, went all the way and compensated with certainty. You lose one of the two people whose duty it is to provide the truth and you replace her with your own vision of the truth. It has to be strong. You look out at the world and say, yes, it must be this or this. On or off. Better that than nothingness and blur. Matters. What matters?

"And you think I'm one of the people who understands that everything matters."

She nodded.

"When have I ever said that to you?"

"I married you, didn't I?" she said.

"If we get a new one," he said, "then we can just start again and invest the damn thing with our own new memories. If that's so important."

"But why do that if there's something better out there already? It's not as though the cradle's gonna fill up with too many memories. I want it."

Matt saw his father-in-law turn with the four hamburgers on a wooden tray and start walking toward them, looking down at the patties. Two of them had cheese. "I don't think you're gonna get it back," Matt said. "I'm sorry. It's gone, sweetheart."

"You don't seem to be understanding," Marissa said, leaning forward as her father set the tray on the table.

She had one hand down on her belly. She was wearing a black maternity top that he'd watched her buy last week. It cost forty-five dollars and Matt spent fifteen minutes standing beside her in the store, trying to talk her out of buying it. She looked beautiful now.

Her black shining hair had grown out in the past year since she'd gotten pregnant. Even in the ponytail, the bangs were evident. They were the bangs that were in style with even younger girls, those Matt had seen at the UWM campus, those that Marissa probably saw when she was at work. Something about all those young girls on their way to a different life made her take their haircuts. When he met her, it was cut short. She had been playing croquet in the middle of the park for some crazy reason, and he'd been sitting on a bench, smoking.

Already the sliced tomatoes, onions, ketchup, and mustard were out on a paper plate. The buns were still in their plastic bag. "Understanding what?" Glen asked softly. He looked at his daughter, then at Matt. "A man goes off to cook hamburgers and suddenly there are secrets?"

Marissa kept looking at Matt, and he understood her look to mean it was up to him to choose whether or not to tell Glen about the request. But this was silly to Matt; either telling him or not would mean he had agreed to the conceit of what his wife suddenly wanted him to do. Out of the blue. As though it were a legitimate request to make. As though she were after pickles. He didn't say anything. He took one of the patties without cheese and made a burger for Marissa with many onions, then squirted ketchup and mustard onto it, all under her watchful eye. After he passed it to her, he took two for himself, one with cheese, one without. As he was making his own, Glen said, "Tornado touched down near La Crosse last night."

"Great, Daddy," said Marissa. "If we lived three hundred miles from here, we might have been sucked away into Oz."

"I'm relating a piece of news about the weather, darling."

She smiled mischievously, bit into her hamburger. This had

been happening. Since she was pregnant, she thought she was allowed to do anything and say anything to anybody. It gave Matt a sense of what she must have been like at fifteen, how difficult for Glen to handle on his own. As she was chewing, she again turned her gaze to Matt. He watched her. Eventually he shook his head and she smiled just a little bit. She had mustard on her lip.

"Sorry, Daddy," she said, turning to him. "I'm cranky."

"Well," said Glen, raising his eyebrows, holding his burger in front of his mouth, looking at the fence at the edge of the yard, "that is not exactly new." He smiled, then looked to her, then looked to Matt, making sure that his idea of a very funny joke did not cause anybody pain.

Matt felt out of sorts as he did the dishes. Marissa had gone upstairs to lie down and Glen was in the living room on the sofa, watching television and sipping a beer. Matt had his own beer on the countertop beside the dish caddy, and between rounds he set the scrub brush down in the sink and raised the beer to his lips. She was plainly not joking. And he knew she would not forget about it. Other people he knew would forget about it. Other people he knew — all the people he knew — got ideas in their heads from time to time about doing something that mattered. A chance came to do something that fit well into the story of your life, and you either had the choice to take it or not take it. He even had that feeling, once in a while, but he let go, too. The difference was that ninety-nine-point-nine-nine-nine percent of the other people let that feeling go after about fifteen minutes. His wife would not.

The best example of it happening to him was a moment when he'd suddenly decided it was important for him to find his parents. He was twenty-two, and he had been grinding away at work at

Delco for three solid years. He'd never thought much about finding them before. Sometime around age seven or eight he just told himself he had no natural parents, and until that moment playing pool with Eric Granderson and the Reilly brothers, he had continued to believe it, as though it were a truth akin to gravity. They just didn't exist. He was delivered by a stork. But that night, as he leaned down with the cue resting on his fingers, sizing up a split at the other end of the table, the whole invisible big idea blocking his way vanished, and before he even took the shot — he missed — he realized he had to find them. There were too many questions. There was too much history and too much pain caused by their whispering departure to let them escape so easily. He spent a week calling foster homes and then an adoption agency. At times it felt like it was going to work, and his enthusiasm kept moving forward. As did his fear. Then he hit a wall: an answering machine. The sound of a woman's voice saying she was away from her desk, but please leave a message. He did. Many times. Over and over again. Ma'am, hello, my name is Matthew Bishop, I'm calling to inquire about some time I spent in a few different foster homes and I'd also like any information you might have about who might have given me up for adoption originally. Far more formal than how he ever talked — he'd even written the speech down on a slip of paper before the third call. But no answer came. So he'd backtracked and called the others again, and they'd given him this woman's number again. Betsy something. Betsy Middlebrook? He left more messages. Maybe four. Ma'am, hello, my name is Matthew Bishop.

Then one morning he woke up and decided he was done, all of the energy to pursue his parents was out of his system. It had left him like the heat of a fire leaving a chimney, entering the cold.

He'd tried, and besides, he didn't need them. He had worked long enough and made enough to be comfortable inside a world with huge gaps of not knowing. It had been a crazy idea. A foolish idea. A child's. He went back to living his life.

Marissa wasn't the same way. Marissa just kept going when she wanted something. Just like the black shirt. She waited him out and won the argument, not because Matt decided he thought it was a good idea but because he realized the total cost of resisting the shirt was greater than forty-five dollars.

Finished with the dishes, Matt stood in the kitchen near the stairwell and picked his battle. Either upstairs to Marissa, where her cradle-plan urgings would probably continue, or into the living room to watch TV with his father-in-law. He didn't recall inviting Glen to stay and watch TV. That sort of invitation was never required with Glen, actually. But Matt had a special place for Glen because of the way he made himself at home. He was now fifty-seven years old and worked in the administrative offices of a soap factory in the middle of Milwaukee. He'd been on the floor when he was younger but had worked his way up through the years, and then, when he'd gotten arthritis in his knees, he'd worked his way across, into the administrative offices.

Matt went into the room and sat down on the sofa with him. "Great burgers, Dad," he said to Glen. "You know how to work that thing."

"Thank you," Glen said softly, still watching the television.

Matt noticed how low the volume was on the TV.

Glen had some kind of cop show on. The volume was so low that the voices were like whispers. This was not normal. Matt looked over at Glen. Glen said, "She had a sister, you know."

"Who?"

"Caroline," Glen said, turning to him. "She had a sister. Marissa doesn't know this. If you want to find Caroline, or the cradle, the best I can do is point you toward her sister. She lives in Sturgeon Bay."

Matt kept staring at Glen.

He was not about to deny the conversation he'd had outside, but he was having trouble understanding how Glen had heard it at all.

"You become a superhero since the last time I saw you?" Matt asked him.

Glen smiled. "I've still got my tricks," he said.

He set the remote control down on the coffee table, then very gingerly reached up to his ear, dug around for a moment, and withdrew his finger. Matt leaned over and peered at the insect-like object Glen held out for him. It was a tiny flesh-colored hearing aid, so small that neither Marissa nor he had noticed it all evening.

"You know, they actually fit these things right into each person's particular ear hole?" Glen said.

"No," Matt said. "I didn't."

"Well, they do. I got this one on Wednesday. I've been having a little trouble with it, however."

"How so?"

"Volume seems to be set too high," Glen said, and he started laughing. "I spent all Thursday blowing my head up every time I tapped the damned computer keyboard. It was like a war was starting."

"Isn't that something," Matt said.

Glen nodded, then sighed, replacing the hearing aid.

"Her sister," he said again, "lives in Sturgeon Bay. It's her half sister, actually. You can find something out there about the cradle, I would guess. Maybe even Caroline's there, too."

"And you never went looking for her yourself? Knowing this?"

"No."

"How do you know she's even alive?"

"I don't. I don't care if she's alive." He stayed still for a long time, and Matt, despite the urge to do it, felt it would not be right to say anything else. Glen looked lost inside of something big and deep, a cavern Matt could not accompany him through, so he turned back to the television and watched cops talking to one another. He couldn't hear them.

"Matt," said Glen finally.

Matt turned. His father-in-law was looking at the magazines on the table. The cop show was invisible.

"If you do go — and I'm not saying you should go or not go — but if you do go, and if somehow you find her, please do me one favor."

"Okay."

Glen turned his head from the magazines and finally looked at Matt directly. "Please tell Caroline I say hello."

Upstairs, twenty minutes after Glen waved good-bye to his daughter, just one hand through the crack in the bedroom door, Matt sat on the edge of the bed and looked down at his wife. She had taken a bowl of ice cream with her, which she'd finished and set on the bedside table. He looked at the remains of the vanilla and a curl of something else, maybe caramel, at the bottom of the bowl. The spoon was propped up inside. Marissa was watching television, one of the evening talk shows, and Matt watched it with her quietly for a few minutes. When a commercial came on, he said, "Are you serious?"

"I am serious," she said, not moving her neck but flicking her eyes to him and watching him carefully. There was still some ice cream around her mouth. She'd changed into her pajamas but was outside the covers.

He looked down at her feet, and while he looked at them, she wiggled her toes.

"Because I'll find it for you," he said. "If you are. So help me. Don't start me on things unless you want them to be finished." He turned back to her and smiled. He liked to think of himself this way, as an unstoppable force. Of course, there was the matter of the answering machine.

"I would like that very much."

"This is my last try to talk you out of it."

"Okay," she said. "Go ahead."

"Marissa," he said. "We're going to have a baby. I think that's just about all the meaning I require."

"He's bringing it out in me," she said, her hand going to her belly. Together they looked at it. "He's making me think about her."

"That makes sense," Matt said.

"Yeah. It does."

"If I get it," he said, "and bring it back here, what is that going to show you? It's an object. We're here. We have our home. We have everything we could need. It's going to be fine when he comes. Is that it?"

"Do you know what you want to name him yet?" she asked, not bothering to answer or disguise that she wasn't going to.

"What about Ty?"

"That was my dog's name when I was little."

"Oh."

"Besides," she said, "that's a redneck name. And not even from here. Isn't that from the South? 'Hey, Tyrone.'" She said the last words in her approximation of a Southern accent. Matt smiled and leaned toward her and let his mouth hover near hers.

"That," he said, in his own drawl, "was the worst Southern accent I've ever heard." He knew his was better, even though it still wasn't very good. But the difference in quality was enough to make both of them laugh.

"So," she said, after he kissed her and sat back up, "you'll try?"

"You've given me no other option."

"You could just say no," she said.

"I know I could," he said, "as you are crazy. Any jury of rational minds would side with me."

"Good thing this trial isn't going to court, then."

"Good thing."

He left her with the television on and went downstairs to finish cleaning up. When he was done, he took a beer outside, wandered through his small backyard for a minute or so, then drifted to the grill, which he scrubbed with the steel brush halfheartedly, still sipping at the beer. The sound scraped its way out into the night neighborhood. He sat down in one of the lawn chairs and looked into his neighbor's backyard, then up at the stars. It was a new moon — the sky was crisp and black and the stars were fairly strong, at least in the west. To the east the glow of Milwaukee lit up the lower part of the sky like a spilled glass of lemonade. He looked back down and saw Frank Rosenblum in the kitchen next door, wearing a white T-shirt. He was in his boxer shorts, looking through his refrigerator. It looked like 1947 inside his house.

Last winter his wife died of pancreatic cancer. Matt had watched warily from the yard as the illness moved on, had seen snapshots through the window like a magic lantern and stitched them together into a story with reports from Marissa, who often went through the gate after supper to sit with Mrs. Rosenblum and have tea. Matt, for the life of him, could not imagine what those conversations had been, the specific details. As winter moved on and Mrs. Rosenblum faded, he began to understand that his wife was pursuing the answers to dark questions of her own, but again, just as he'd felt with Glen earlier, he knew she'd be the only one able to understand. They had only just moved in and hardly knew their neighbors, but she'd gone, over and over again, all the way up to the night Mrs. Rosenblum died.

A few weeks later, in March, Matt had spoken with Frank across the fence about Frank's plans to trim the apple tree that hung over into their yard. Frank apologized profusely, and Matt told him not to worry about it, they didn't mind at all. Frank thanked him. Then Frank simply cut the entire tree down one rainy evening. Matt stood in the kitchen, watching through the window, as the old man cut through the tree in one slice of the chain saw, then sliced it into smaller pieces, then hauled them around the house to the curb. He remembered the sound of the chain saw's little engine going right alongside the rain on the roof. The stump of the tree, exactly one foot high, was still there.

2

She awoke and slipped from bed at 5:15 a.m. The house was quiet, empty, dark. As she made the coffee, Renee Owen looked through the window to the frozen black morning in their backyard. The thermometer outside the window, itself caked in ice, read nine degrees.

She looked away from the red vertical line and back to the dark snow. It was an odd thing to think, but it didn't take much to see the cold. It was supposed to be invisible, but there it was, right there. You could hear it, too, in the wind, and maybe even smell it in the heat blowing from the vents in the floor. Without the sun, she guessed the waving foot of snow in their backyard had turned solid. She imagined walking across the top of it without breaking through. She imagined being barefoot, feeling the hard ice on the bottoms of her feet. It was warm inside, but she imagined herself out there, freezing, stepping gingerly.

For an hour she sat alone in the big chair in the den, reading.

Bill wandered down the stairs at 6:45, the hair on the sides of his head sticking out horizontally.

"Is he coming?" Bill asked her, squinting.

"He said he'd come at nine."

Their son was going to war. This was the week he would disappear and become an idea. It sounded impossible and it was absolutely true. Renee had hoped for months she would find the magic key, even as her desperation expanded, but in the end the hope was hollow and perfunctory. She'd gone to his apartment and they'd had long, intelligent adult dialogues at his kitchen table. There was the case of Vietnam to consider, and besides Vietnam, there was the more present sense that the war in Iraq already was lost, that nobody was for it, not really. He humored her. She cried. He humored her. She called him and told him about an article she'd read and begged until her own voice, in her ear, was nothing more than a child's. Fifty-eight, and this was turning her into a baby. He humored her again; he told her he'd be fine. His calm and arrogant nineteen-year-old way of trying to appease her didn't properly match her anger, and it made it all the worse. His ideas were equally infuriating ("If I live in this country and get to have this great life, I should be ready to fight for it, too, right?"), and his insouciance ("I don't get what the big deal is anyway") was youthful, cold, thoughtless. It reminded her of the past.

Bill went to take a shower and Renee went to their room and took off her bathrobe and got dressed. She read more, Bill read the newspaper. She drifted off and woke up and made coffee again. The doorbell rang just before nine o'clock, and Adam, bundled, smiled at the door and gave her a hug.

"There he is," Bill said when he came into the room, and Adam laughed for no reason.

They all went to the kitchen and had more coffee.

She had spent a good part of nineteen years trying to do or say whatever a mother might do or say to build up all the kinds of thinking and ways of looking at the world that would keep a son from waking up one day, deciding there wasn't any other choice to make, walking down, signing papers, and flying off, armed to the teeth, to do the work of government. With Vietnam it was so different. Then, it was easy to say the war was the wrong thing, almost fashionable to say it, especially in the city of Days of Rage and the Democratic National Convention, especially in the house of two professor parents. Here and now, today, 2008, so many of those old lines were crisscrossed, weren't they? The way people thought was different. Was it that no one cared? No, that wasn't it, not exactly. But something close. Something like: it doesn't matter. It will turn out on its own. So let's just hang out.

In only forty years that had happened. They'd been so confused then and they were still so confused, but at least then their confusion had been tilted in the right direction, the direction in which things mattered.

You will die, Renee had even said to her son. You will die in that godforsaken place, Adam. I am begging you. You think you'll be fine, but I see very clearly the point you're trying to make and it's not worth it.

Since then, she'd stopped speaking of doom directly. But she felt it. Really she knew from the morning they'd watched the towers fall down. She remembered. She and Bill both sitting there in the living room, Adam already at school. The building buckled and the unreal finale began. Exactly at that moment, some dark aspect of her heart awoke and shook its head at her and tsked its finger back and forth and said, Don't you understand? And she did. It fit her history perfectly and to her it seemed designed and implemented from above. It was a punishment.

She knew everything in advance. As they watched the towers on television, she knew Bill's thoughts. She could see them. He stood quietly in the living room, wearing his suit, staring at the screen, car keys still in his hand. Briefcase there on the floor, leaning against the couch. Something like: all those Arabs now must pay, damn them to hell! As though it could be erased. And as she watched her husband, she saw more: it would slip from his mind into Adam's, from father to son. She could guess about the announcements coming over the PA at Adam's school, too. She could guess how they would say it. She could imagine all the years of the country's anger that would come, imagine the whole shift of feeling that would overtake their street and their suburb and the restaurants and buses, seep all through Chicago, to all of the Midwest, to the South, to the coasts, seep into every person, no matter who they were. Not bloodlust but uncertainty. And with that came anything.

And Adam. When she became Prometheus that morning in the living room, she saw his whole path as well. No one remembered that about Prometheus — he was a seer, not just a thief, not just the demigod chained to the rock and eaten. She saw the future just as he had. The world would bristle, war would come, and Adam would go toward it. She saw it and knew it would be true. He was only twelve years old, but she knew him well enough, even then. He would look at every person who said, no, it's wrong, and he would say, no, you're wrong. And he would look at every person who said, yes, it's right, and he would say, maybe it is; maybe it's right, maybe it's not. I'm going to see for myself because I, unlike you, am not afraid.

That was Adam's way. He knew he could be unique in the world if he guessed at what other people feared and then immediately did that very thing. Every play battle, in one blink of his child's mind's eye, would shimmer and become human and real. In an instant he could move past every one of his friends and every one of his classmates and be standing alone. Except he could not possibly understand what that meant. At twelve years old or nineteen years old, he could not understand what that meant.

"I feel like donuts," Adam said.

"Donuts?"

"I know Daddy Warbucks feels like donuts. What does the ol' champion say?"

Renee wasn't watching this exchange. Her back was to them both. Now the sun had come up and the snow in the backyard was glaring bright. The sense of their Illinois home being an absolute arctic wasteland had faded some, and now it even appeared beautiful to Renee, in some abstract way. In some alternate universe, this exact family is on their way out to go ice-skating together, she thought. She felt gray and numb. She was at the sink, looking down at the bits of onion and dill that had collected in the drain guard.

She reached her finger down and started scooping up what she could.

"Then, let's have them," she heard Bill say. "I'm no anti-donutist."

She turned.

"Okay, my boys. Let's have them, I agree," she said. "Should I go? Why don't I just bring them back?"

"We can all go," Adam said. "Isn't that weird? To imagine actually, like, sitting down at Dunkin' Donuts?"

Adam laughed. He had stripped his layers down and was now wearing only jeans and a white T-shirt. He'd already buzzed his hair once, which had upset her. It had grown out a little since and he hadn't done it again. Still, it was only fuzz. Beneath his light stubble his cheeks were rosy, and she could still see the twelve-year-old boy in his long face. Now, she admitted, it was a man's face, not a boy's — strong cheekbones and a strong jaw, considerate and expectant eyes. He was athletic, he looked strong. But when he looked at her, she saw the child first, then what was real.

"That sounds like a fun adventure," she said.

Bill just stared.

"Let's all go," she said, nodding. "I think it'll be nice. I haven't eaten a donut in about five years."

For a moment the two watched her at the sink.

"You're totally not into this," Adam said. "It's fine."

"I am," she said. "Really."

"I do like the fake positivity, Mom."

"It's not fake," she said. "It's not."

"Eating donuts here, at home, is also interesting," Bill said. "To me. Incidentally. Do you two realize what it's like out there?"

Adam stepped sideways; he stood directly behind his father. She watched as he ceremoniously placed his hand on the skin of Bill's bald head. Adam started rubbing back and forth. Bill didn't bother turning around and looking up. This had happened before. It was their routine.

"What does the genie tell you?" Bill asked, still holding his coffee cup.

"The genie tells me that your attitude about the donuts," Adam said, "sucks ass."

"What else does it say?"

"The genie says you want to go out, not stay here."

"All right, all right," Bill said, pushing Adam's hand away. "Let's go sit at Dunkin' Donuts, then. Like every family should."

Adam had taken quite a shine to what this week was becoming: anything he wanted. It reminded Renee of how he'd been at Christmas a decade ago. All the usual things — unable to sleep, obsessed with his presents, Santa Claus. Wanting to camp on the roof to see. But his enthusiasm for the holiday ran deeper than it did for other children, she knew. The idea of *gift*, of *present*. Of getting when it was not asked and giving when it was not asked. She had seen his fascination with it over the years. The transition of things — that was his obsession.

Was it such a stretch to say this same feeling was what drew him to Iraq? No clear idea of what he would be giving but the sense that it was, asked for or unasked for, another gift? If so, if that was really it, then she was sorry, he was her son but he was an idiot. The blurred lines infuriated her. He had probably heard some blustering man on CNN one day say something about the gift of freedom and used that to make up his mind.

As she slid her coat over her shoulders and found her hat, she thought that this was the perfect paradox of parenting: they ignored every lesson you taught and instead found lessons you had never thought to teach and made them their own. They got them somewhere, picked them up, looked at them like they were shiny baubles on the side of the road — they understood that they were not their parents' laws and not their history's laws, so they made them their own. For freedom's sake. Or maybe just to survive.

She looked in the mirror and brushed her hair aside, tucking a clump of bangs beneath the elastic of the maroon wool. She did not feel old. She was fifty-eight years old and she felt forty-two, and she'd felt forty-two since she'd turned forty-two. She'd had Adam at thirty-nine. So late the doctors had been concerned. Bill had not wanted any children. Neither had she. But she'd woken up one summer day in 1988 and realized she'd been wrong, and she'd said to Bill she was wrong, and he'd thought and had said, finally, okay, I understand. We'll have one. We can do this — at least we've got the money now, huh? Renee had thought: when did we ever not have the money?

She didn't look old. Good skin, her mother always said. You have good skin, absolutely unlike mine. Renee was glad for whatever genetic anomaly made it possible. Now, adjusting her hair, she felt what she always felt when she looked at her face — glad it was her own but surprised this was the thing that stood her place in the world and showed people it was she.

Here is me, she thought.

"Ready?"

"I'm ready."

Dunkin' Donuts wouldn't have been too difficult a walk, but it had snowed overnight, then frozen over, and the sidewalks weren't clear. She waited beside Adam in the snow as Bill backed the car out of the garage. The air was cold but not unbearable. She let it come down into her lungs and meet with the warmth of her body. She imagined it down there, swirling.

"It's cold, huh?" Adam said.

The garage door was coming up. Adam put his arm over his mother's shoulder and squeezed her once, quickly, as though to warm the air in her lungs. It meant more. She knew it was his way of trying to apologize. He'd done it over and over again these last weeks, made small apologies. Replacing the batteries of the smoke detector as an I'm sorry, sweeping out the garage as an I'm sorry.

He couldn't say it out loud, because he didn't actually mean it, but he could give invisible apologies that were just apologies for making her so afraid.

"It is," she said, tightening her shoulders at his touch. "Yes. Brrr."

"Mom," he said, looking down at her. "Come on."

"What?"

"I can tell you don't feel good. It's obvious."

"Can you?"

He looked at the white lights of the car as it crept from the garage. "Just don't get all weird. I'm leaving in a couple —"

"Weird is a lazy word, Adam. Don't you dare use it on me."

"You know what I mean."

"I do," she said, "and you know what I mean, and we're going to get donuts. I'm fine." She twisted her head and looked up at him. "Is that weird?"

"No," he said.

"I'm fine."

"Okay," he said, taking his arm away. "You're not, but okay."

They drove down the street, just a half mile, Adam in the back, his knees up awkwardly, Bill leaning forward and being careful on the slippery roads. She tried to find the word Adam hadn't been able to find as they sat in an orange booth at Dunkin' Donuts. She didn't know why, but she didn't remove her coat or hat as they ate. Perhaps it was the urge to flee at a moment's notice. Both Bill and Adam did remove their coats. They hung on the hooks attached to their booth. Dunkin' Donuts, she thought. I have never, she thought, actually been in a Dunkin' Donuts. It was down the street from the house she'd lived in for fifteen years, and she'd driven past it nearly every day. She'd walked by it, she'd stared at the bubble lettering. She'd looked through the glass at people chomping down. Still, this was the first time she'd ever been inside.

She ate one donut and they each ate four; they had coffee and she had water in a Styrofoam cup. As they talked she looked out the half-frosted window at the whitened street, saw cars sliding here and there, and thought: not weird but displaced. Not weird but discord. Not weird but unexpected. Not weird but inharmonious. Not weird but improper. Not weird but juxtaposed.

"— still going to Hawaii, then?" Adam was saying.

She turned back to them. Adam stared at her. Bill, also, looked and waited.

"Are we still going?" she said. "Is that what you're asking?"

"Yes."

She looked at her husband. "I don't know. Are we? Have we decided? I thought all this was all on hold."

"I think we're going," Bill said, pushing his chin down in what Renee had always taken to be something he did in meetings. "All things considered. We need sun. Both of us."

They'd had the plan for a year, longer than they'd known that Adam would be leaving. The idea of the trip, now, to Renee, was repulsive. Vacations were unethical. Adam was going to the desert to be killed to prove a point about the upper middle class's dedication to democracy, and they would be lying on a beach, tanning, while it happened.

She was the one to plan it and now she would rather die than go to Hawaii.

"I do need it," she said. "I do need a break, it's true."

She would find some other way to kill the trip after Adam was gone. Her fear of flying would overwhelm her the week before.

"You'll get it," Bill said. He patted Adam on the shoulder. "Next year, kiddo, you come, too. Try to have a wife with you, okay? Or at least a girlfriend?"

"Yeah, right," Adam said, smiling widely, and Renee looked at the smile and thought: you are a child.

She turned away from them. Through the window she saw a mother pushing a stroller. She caught the slightest glimpse of a puffy blue hood ringed with fur inside and imagined the baby sitting upright, eyes open, taking in the cold and snow. Some little boy having his first taste of what it was like when the elements became disagreeable. The mother was dressed in brown fashionable clothes and had a black stocking cap on. She looked rich. Bill and Adam again dropped into their own conversation, and Renee scraped a piece of frosting from her fingernail. All she had to do was check in once in a while. She knew that. She was allowed her leeway. Adam could get donuts on Saturday morning and she could stare out the window while it happened. They all agreed that she would drift off here and there.

And why shouldn't I? she wondered. Here, here, I make this choice, good-bye. Then she could daydream. She could think about what she would write later on. She could form phrases, crack them apart, lock them back together. She could do whatever she wanted if they could do whatever they wanted.

She looked at the plowed piles of snow up against the curb — there was one mound in particular that seemed to be almost a perfect pyramid, and someone had made the decision to place a snowball at the peak. She hoped it would snow again tonight, that they would all be able to sit together in the living room after supper and they would all be able to glance up, from time to time, through the windows and see the white dropping down, and that way, they would all know — that way, there would be one more thing. She imagined it: black-orange sky, white snow. Maybe even red fire in the living room. If she was allowed to make a memory, right here, today, that would be exactly it. If God reached down and handed her a sack with every single thing inside of it and told her she was allowed to make just one memory from the ingredients, whether or not it happened, whether or not it was real, that would be exactly it.

It didn't snow again. Instead of staying home, Adam decided to go bowling with his friends.

It was Saturday night and he was leaving on Wednesday. He promised to come again tomorrow, watch football with his father, and afterward stay for dinner. Now Bill was on the couch, glasses low on his nose, engrossed in an episode of *Mystery!* She watched it with him for five minutes but decided to go to the office and look over her manuscript.

She was on to structure — the poems were finished, nearly — it was just a matter of arranging them. She had set up a bulletin board on the wall with the title of every poem written on a white note card. This way she could stand in front of the whole thing and see it laid out all in one shot, and she could mix and match by theme, image, content. The only thing she felt sure of was that there would be two parts — so often the chapbooks were divided into thirds, as though all books of poetry were syllogisms. She was tired of that logic and wanted something else.

Two parts felt right. It was something like: there is a before and there is an after. There is a yes and there is a no. There is a now and there is a then. The world is separated into two parts.

Now and then was right because she'd not been a poet, not

in her mind, for thirty-some years. Poetry started her writing, but she'd had access to something else when she was young, something elemental and angry and burning that faded out of her heart. By the time she met and married Bill, at thirty, it was gone. By then she'd already moved to children's books and sold three. Now, at fifty-eight, she was the author of more than a dozen. She was Renee Owen. She was the smiling lady on the back of the book. She was the lady who had written it, you see? She wasn't famous but she was read, most definitely. She had done well. And it didn't bother her that she was not the best-known children's writer of the century. That was not important. What delighted her was the secret cadre of children who carried her stories along with them in their minds, whether they knew it or not. There were thousands of them.

Whether they knew it or not, they were out there, an entire army, some of them now grown. She helped make their minds and their imaginations, their rights and their wrongs, every single one. Who were they? Where were they? It didn't matter, and she would never know, but they carried along Fiona and Samuel, the sister and brother detectives; they carried along Wesley, the ape; they carried the prince named Thomas on the quest to find his shield; and they carried along the kittens and the yubyubs and the evil men who came to tell Annabelle her parents had given her up.

That voice, though — that voice that woke up and whispered in her ear on 9/11 — that was the thing. That was what had left her all the way back then, in 1969. She'd thought it was simply gone forever, that Jonathan's death was the death of some space within her own heart, the same space where that voice lived. The evil surprise was that it was back, a reborn child and full-grown by the time Adam came home and announced his plans to be a marine. On that day, she decided there would be no more children's books. She was through with them. And from there, it was only a matter of time before the poems began to come back. Only words and phrases in the night at first, as she drifted off to sleep, and later, whole stanzas that came to her at dinner with Bill's decrepit parents or while she gripped the wheel and listened to NPR and waited for the wax coating in the car wash.

She had a whole book — forty-nine poems. The book frightened her. There was no saying what the poems were. There were few characters, rarely any complete human forms. War, and fear of war, and fear of loss from war. But there were other phrases and lines that did not make sense to her at all. Each one of the cards correlated to one of the poems, and the poems were printed and stacked in a pile on the desk. She ran her eyes across the right-hand group of cards, focused on one. Then she went to her papers and flipped through the stack until she found what she was looking for.

The truth was, she had no idea what she was doing with any of the poems, and she had no idea whether she would try to publish them, or what she would try to do. She replaced "Wednesday's Child" in the stack, stepped back, and looked at the board. Some of them she'd shown to Bill. Only a handful. He'd read them and he'd been very kind. A few times she asked him to tell her more — more about what they made him see in his mind, more about what they made him feel. He had tried to respond. It was not his strong suit, this kind of thing. He was better at the stock market. He was better at taxes and finding property to buy. Snow-blowing. She no longer had any poet friends. The only other reader she could go to was her mother, but so far she hadn't been able to do it. Her mother's readings would be the opposite of Bill's.

Her mother's readings would be too deep. Her mother knew too much. Her mother would see what the metaphors pointed to in the world.

She focused on another card, tacked up on the board but far off to the side, not included in either category. There was one word written on it.

APOLOGY

This poem didn't exist. It was the only card that didn't connect to something she'd actually written.

This poem was still inside her. She didn't know what it would be or how it would look. She doubted she would ever write it. But there it was on the board, interestingly enough.

Right now the poem was only a feeling — not a single image attached to it. She knew it fit into the whole somewhere, but she wasn't ready to ask how, to sit down and try to see. When she imagined the poem, she only felt worried; a cold wind, a dark, lost feeling. Herself, or someone, in a cave. Nothing to do but wait and hope.

She knew, as she knew every single day of her life, what the apology was for. She hadn't made herself that blind, not yet. It was for what she had done. For Jonathan, long dead. But there were other questions. Who would see it? Who would overhear it, and what would that mean? Could it be told? Who would know it was there, and what would that do? Would she then have to go out and deliver it? And if it ever became more than only a card, what then? Even seeing how the A and the Os and the G and the Y fit together as they did made her stomach drop. She knew the power and could feel it. She knew it was bigger than she was, that it could destroy her as easily as a crashing wave could lift a healthy human body and drop it and batter it against the sand and the coral and be done with it, then recede, all in one second, leaving a wet corpse behind.

She was terrified of it.

However, there was the card.

She expected to find Bill asleep on the couch downstairs. When she came into the living room, she saw that he was still awake, sitting upright in front of the television. No more *Mystery!* He was watching the news.

"Hi," he said, looking up. "Bedtime for the old people?"

"Yes," she said, coming to the couch. "I'm absolutely exhausted." She flopped down beside him. His arm came instinctively around her. With his other hand, Bill adjusted his glasses. The weather was on, and he said, "They think more snow tomorrow."

"Maybe it will just snow permanently," she said. "Forever."

"For that," he said, "we may have to get a new snowblower."

She breathed out, looked up at the ceiling. "You are so calm," she said.

"I'm not calm," he said. "I look calm. I'm scared, too, Renee."

"I don't even look calm," she said.

"Well," Bill said, "you're the mother. Something would be wrong if you looked calm."

"He chose it. Of all the things that make no sense about this. He *chose* it. This is *our* child."

Bill didn't react to this. She wanted to make it seem like it was impossible that their child would become this. Obviously it wasn't. She had her thoughts about children choosing other paths and finding their own ways, but there was also this: Bill was Bill. Bill had never said a thing to indicate he was against war in general, or against this one in particular. What if he had been firm? He was diplomatic and not aggressive. He had a balanced opinion on the subject and saw merits here and there. He was patriotic when it was convenient and he didn't get tired, ever, of making fun of Hillary Clinton. He was a fungible man and hadn't pushed Adam hard one way or the other.

She wanted to hate him for it and to see this way he had as weakness, and yet here, now, beside him, she felt no resentment. Only loss, and fear. Love for him, love for the years of life they had together. She thought of the APOLOGY card.

Maybe it was for him, after all. Maybe she'd guessed wrong. How was it possible to live with one man for this many years and never, ever mention to him the central truth of your history, the one most important thing? He knew about Jonathan, of course. Some old boyfriend, a tragic story. But he didn't know everything. She dreaded what he would feel if he ever knew. He would feel like he didn't know her. He would look at the same face she'd studied in the mirror this morning and it would go from familiar to alien in a flash. She would see it as it happened, and it would be unbearable. For most of their marriage, she had assumed she would just die and never say a thing for fear of that moment. The secret was so old, so a part of her, that the thought now — the voice? — surprised her. It said: you know you can tell him, don't you? Even though? Just tell him.

She looked at the television and saw apocalypse. The images were of a fire, from above. Some industrial building, sprawling, was engulfed in flames.

Around it were what seemed to be thousands of fire trucks and police cars, all their lights flashing. Mobs of people made of tiny colored dots were grouped together in clumps not far from the building.

Bill must have felt her muscles tense up, because he turned to her and studied her face, squinted, and said, "What?"

"Nothing," she said. "This just" — she nodded at the TV — "this just looks horrible. What is it?"

"Mmm," Bill said, looking back. "Chemical plant, I think," he said. "Yesterday afternoon. It's up near Milwaukee. A whole bunch of people died."

"What happened?"

"Look at it," he said. "It burned."

"It looks just... terrible."

Bill nodded again. "It was, from what I've heard. Very bad. Ammonia compressor exploded." He frowned down at the remote control, then pointed it at the TV and turned the volume up. The sound of the reporter's voice filled the room. She was speaking of the dead.

"Delco," Bill said. "Delco, I believe that place is called."

3

Matt took a change of course on Monday and began trying to divvy his Delco shifts instead of collect them. When Ken Granderson, Eric's father, wandered into the break room, Matt offered him up Friday and he took it. To be on the safe side, he found Eric a little later and got him to take Thursday, then went to talk to the foreman to make sure all was understood. There was a funeral in Tennessee he had to go to. Old friend from grade school who'd moved away. Gun accident, tragedy. Okay, Bishop, the foreman had said kindly. I understand.

On Wednesday night he changed the oil in the truck and made sure the windshield wipers were fine, drove it to the gas station, filled it up, bought three Twinkies, put them in the glove compartment, and went home. He and Marissa tried to have sex, but for the last few weeks it had been too uncomfortable, even from behind, as they had grown accustomed to.

"I'm sorry," she said as he got out of bed and crossed the room, toward the bathroom.

He said, "It's fine," turned on the shower, stuck his head back out, and said, "It's fine," again, then went into the shower and masturbated with his back to the curtain, listening hard to make sure she wouldn't sneak in and surprise him.

Glen had produced an address. Matt had it written down and stuffed into his wallet, although, really, he didn't need anything. The half sister's name was Mary and the address was 78 9th Avenue. Glen had a little tickle in his voice when he told him over the phone. Matt said, "Not only did you never go to look."

"It's hard to forget an address like that."

"That address is so easy I'm surprised you didn't just one day suddenly find yourself there."

"I'm not."

"Glen," Matt said, "are you and Caroline still married, then?"

"No. The papers came in the mail a few months later. Some lawyer in Minneapolis. I signed them all and sent them back where they were supposed to go, and that was the end."

"Why'd you sign them?" Matt asked. "Couldn't you have found her that way? Gone to see her? Talked to her?"

"I signed them —" Glen started saying, but he hesitated. Matt waited. "I signed them just because. Maybe this is hard to understand, but I signed them because I thought signing them would make three lives better. Every life inside of the family."

"What family?"

"Ours."

"But it was gone."

"Yes," he said. "Yes."

"Does Marissa know about the papers?"

"Yes," he said. "She knows."

In the morning Matt had cereal at the table in the kitchen.

Marissa came down while he was eating, in her bathrobe. She'd called in sick. He didn't think she should be working anymore anyway, but Marissa, up until now, had done everything she could to continue and seemed almost offended by the idea of changing her routine or her life. She didn't want anyone to think she was taking advantage.

"No one's gonna think that," Matt had said. "You work at the damned Planned Parenthood. They live for people like you. I'm surprised they haven't bought you a new car for getting pregnant."

"I know," she'd said. "I just don't want to. After, fine. Then I'll stay home. Before, no."

When he was finished with his cereal, Matt stood in the middle of the kitchen, hands on his hips, and said, "Okay. I'm going."

"You're going where?" she said, surprised.

"I'm going going," he said, raising his eyebrows at her.

"What?" she said, eyes wide now. "You know somewhere to go? Already? For the cradle?"

He nodded.

"How?"

"You said you didn't want to know."

"And what were you planning to do? Just disappear for a couple of days? Just slip out on me?"

"Do you want the thing or not, Marissa? It might only take me a day. I don't know."

"See?" she said, snapping her fingers at him. "You do know how to do it. Right away. Like the keys. You're fucking magic is what you are."

"Call me a genius."

She stood up, and he gave her a hug, then rubbed her belly

and knelt down and said good-bye to it. "Genius," said Marissa from above.

"See you soon, Tyrone," he said to her stomach. He stood up. "See you soon. I'll call."

She smiled the same smile she always smiled. Matt thought of the moment from the day in the park, when he'd met his wife. He had taken to going there that spring, for no reason he understood. What had been years of watching television in the evening suddenly morphed into a stroll down to St. Helens Park to sit on the bench, smoke, watch children play, or watch people have their barbecues on the old rusted grills provided by the city. Maybe it was something about outdoors versus indoors. Maybe it was just the garbage on TV. He even sat there alone in the snow one night — it was the middle of April, and the storm was unexpected, but the temperature was just on the edge of freezing, and the flakes came down fat and wet, so they hadn't bothered him in the least. He sat alone, letting the snowflakes land on the shoulders of his jean jacket and watching them from the corner of his eye, melting. The evening he met Marissa was a Thursday. Someone had launched her green striped ball away from the field of play and toward Matt, and amid the hoots and hollers of the group, she'd begrudgingly followed it with her mallet, dragging the thing in the grass. As she waited for her turn and plotted out what direction to shoot, Matt tried to look off at something else, his heart pounding because of how close she was. He could feel her standing there. Before her shot, she looked at him and smiled and said, "Hello. I usually don't find myself so far out of position."

As he moved north of Milwaukee on 43, *Gazetteer* resting on the passenger seat and open to the Door County page, Matt allowed himself to relax about not being at work. He'd been worried about it since the beginning of the week, calculating lost wages and subtracting them from his planned savings. All for a whim. Or something.

At the very least, he was on a drive. At the very least, he could have a day or two to fall out of the typical and stretch. He had no real sense that he required such an escape, but again, these were the reasons he was telling himself it was okay.

He looked to his left, to the west. Somewhat flat and green, somewhat flat and green, but also the yellow of the fields. Wisconsin rolled out to the west, and the sky above was calm. By feeling it through the truck, he knew the wind was blowing. No thunderclouds. Occasionally he'd go by a broken-down farm, the wood so old it was gray. Cows milling, even a few horses running up and down a pasture, chasing one another. Then there would be the newer farms, bright, what he imagined as productive.

There were, he reflected, only three feelings in his heart's repertoire: worry about money, love for Marissa, and a somewhat more mysterious attraction to the simplicity of one single day. There were the typical day-to-day somethings, the colors that turned his head here and there, the annoyances, the reliefs, but those were not the central three. Everyone had those little ones. But then, everyone had a few more that were larger, and their own. Or at least the arrangement was their own. The central three were much larger. Money was money. The Marissa feeling wasn't complicated either; he'd loved her after knowing her for nine days, and ever since then, the feeling had been the same: he would die for her. He would lie down in front of a train and allow himself to be sliced in half for her. She was the best thing that had ever happened to him, and that part was simple. The feeling about the days was farther away but there were times when it approached him in its abstract glory and nearly brought tears to his eyes. What was it? Life? He had no idea. The simple beauty of how the earth rolled and the sun came up and then went down and the sun came up again, how they were allowed to keep doing this, over and over again, thousands upon thousands of times. Asleep awake asleep awake. What he felt was gratitude. He had no interest in poetry or art or music. Something in him, though, told him that whatever the reasons for their existence, it had to do with this same feeling. Gratitude. He didn't need to look at anything or listen to anything to bring on the feeling. Instead, it usually found him. It would come to him at work, and he would take a break; it would come to him when he was driving, and he would even tear up and sometimes even pull over to the side of the road; it would come to him at home, in front of a bad movie or a bad television show, and he would excuse himself and go to the bathroom and sit on the toilet and breathe, leaning forward until it passed. Not that he did not enjoy it. He was embarrassed by this side of himself but he did enjoy it, he did. When it came, it was as though he had one special connection to the world that other people didn't have, so he welcomed it. No one will say no to that.

It wasn't coming now — it was nowhere near. In fact, there was nothing. The only things nearby were the silver chick silhouette tire flaps on the truck in front of him and the bumper and license plate of the little Toyota behind him. Both annoyed him. The Toyota was too close, and the truck in front of him had been altering its speed for the last fifteen miles, first blasting by everyone at seventy-five miles an hour, then slowing up and doing fifty-five in the right lane. The wind was getting it, too, and the trailer was moving with menace to and fro. Matt had passed and then been passed by this same truck at least five times. He wanted to escape it, but no matter what he did, he couldn't. If he slowed, it eventually slowed with him, and if he sped up, it was there. Matt would not have been surprised to pull up alongside it, look up, and see a skeleton driving.

He decided to end the problem completely and get off the road in Sheboygan and eat at an Arby's. Sturgeon Bay was an hour and forty-five minutes away. If he ate now, it was possible that he'd find the sister, find Caroline, and find the cradle all before he was hungry again. He'd be back driving almost immediately and would be home before dark. It felt like he had, in the last week, fallen into a well where time didn't work properly. When had she had the idea? He didn't know. What was the idea? What was it beneath what it appeared to be? He didn't know. How long had she been planning to send him to find it? He didn't know. He didn't know if she'd come up with it on the spot, that day, or if she'd known since she was a girl what she'd send her husband out to do at the last minute. She was capable of either thing. Now, though, for the first time, it occurred to Matt that the request was far more than a whim or an impulse. That Marissa's greatest fear in life was the dissolution of family. That she could not possibly bear to see it happen again. That for her to know it wouldn't, it would take this absurd string of duties accomplished in the eleventh hour. Was she capable of that? He didn't know. Yes. He did know. She was. So now the result was that he felt as though he were inside a well, one without time, where regular life couldn't happen. To get the cradle with miraculous speed — that was the best-case scenario. Of course, it was possible that he wouldn't find anything at all. If he didn't, though, he would just go home and say he'd done what he could, and it was possible that this would satisfy Marissa.

Maybe *possible* wasn't the right word, but it was something.

Inside the Arby's, there were ten or fifteen people at tables here and there, and a few in line, waiting. Matt looked over the menu without paying any attention to it, then looked at the two women at the front of the line, both in their sixties, both upset at the young kid behind the counter. "Does this look like cheese or something else?" one of them said, peeling back the top of the bun of her sandwich and showing the boy. Matt couldn't see what was there. But he did see the boy look down at whatever she was showing him, nod his head slowly, then turn to his manager, a pimple-stained middle-aged woman, and say, "I need another one, and quick."

Matt filled the tank when he was finished eating and veered northeast before Green Bay, heading up toward Sturgeon Bay, listening to talk radio on the AM station.

Seventy-eight 9th Avenue turned out to be a white house with blue shutters and flowers everywhere. Out front, there was an iron bench that looked uncomfortable sitting dappled in sunlight, surrounded by rough beds of wildflowers. The grass had not been mowed in weeks. The yard gave off few signs of interested human control. There was a car in the driveway, and Matt had been sitting in his truck, across the street, for fifteen minutes, looking at the windows and waiting to see whether any shapes passed by. So far he had seen none. All he had seen was a cat in the window staring back out at him, sometimes disappearing for a moment, then reappearing in the same spot. It sat upright, its ears extended, as though straining toward him and probing him with the best of its senses. From time to time, Matt stared straight back at it and tried to send it mental signals: I am not your enemy, I am not your enemy. Then, later: meow.

It was colder than it should have been. It was June, and Matt doubted it was much more than fifty-five degrees. He knew both the lake and the bay were capable of blasting this town, but it surprised him that the difference was so noticeable. His recollections of Door County, which were fuzzy and came from a field trip he'd taken in the eighth grade, didn't fit properly with where he was now. He remembered blazing white homes and condos and small roads; he remembered somewhat confused-looking families of six wandering down the sides of streets in Ephraim, each member holding a plastic bag filled with whatever shopping bounty they'd come away with that day. He remembered sailboats and a feeling of money and he remembered thinking, It's only farmland. Why has this become what it is? It was different here. This was more like a little town where people lived, and it only had a few of the signs that signaled tourist destination. Most of the homes along the road were small and simple, like 78. The only structure noticeably different was a tall, lean bed-and-breakfast across the road, painted orange and red and white, a little gaudy but also grand. A man wearing a straw hat was mowing the lawn, and had been ever since Matt had been parked. In the rearview mirror, Matt took a look at him, then at the roof of the big house, then at the white balcony on the third floor.

Enough, Matt thought, and after rubbing his face, he opened the door of his truck and went to the house. There is a cradle inside this house, he thought.

Weeds came up in the cracks of the walkway, and up in the corners, beneath the roof's overhang and gutters, were whole civilizations of spiders. The webs were layered. Matt got the feeling that if he were up on a ladder and passed his hand through them, he might go all right for a moment but eventually would find himself stuck, along with the insects.

A woman was standing behind the screen door, looking at him. "You like spiders?" she said.

Matt just barely kept himself from jumping back and falling down the stairs. She was a short, round woman, her hair gray and cut almost like a young boy's. She was wearing dark blue jeans and a gray sweatshirt. Her face was gnarled — not wrinkled, exactly, and not from age, exactly. Perhaps from many years of frowning.

"I'm sorry, ma'am," he said.

"Okay. Who are you?"

"I was just coming up here to talk to you and I got distracted, looking at the webs."

"Trust me," the woman said, voice smoke-grizzled. "They're not there because they're pretty."

"My name's Matt Bishop," Matt said. "This is a little bit strange. In fact, I don't even know where to begin."

"Go on," she said, still behind the door. "I do strange."

"I'm looking for somebody. A woman named Mary Landower."

Matt waited to see if it was her. So far there had been no reaction at all. Behind the woman, the cat wandered out into the screened-in porch and sat down at her feet. Matt and it stared at one another for a few seconds; the cat looked pleased it was getting a better look.

"Why'd you sit out there for so long?" said the woman. "In your truck."

"I was collecting myself after the drive."

"Where'd you come from?"

"St. Helens. Near Milwaukee."

"And why do you want her?"

"It's a long story," Matt said. "I'm happy to —"

"You seem to like spiders, however."

"No, ma'am."

"You looked at 'em like you liked 'em."

"I was only looking."

"I'll tell you what," said the woman, pulling the door open and stepping out onto the small porch with him. She looked up now. There was one mean-looking spider in one of the front webs, perfectly still. Matt thought that if you took it down and trained it, you could probably ride it.

"You clean up those webs for me, and I'll tell you where you can find Mary Landower."

"Ma'am."

"I'd say that's a fairly straightforward deal. Are you about to tell me you've got questions?"

"You're not her, I take it."

"No, I'm not her. I knew her when she lived here. I bought this house from her."

"Where is she?"

"You've already used up your questions," said the woman. "There's a broom and a Shop-Vac in the garage. I now have to go get more birdseed."

Okay. Matt cleaned the spiderwebs out while the woman was gone. No matter how out of the ordinary it was, he guessed this would lead somewhere. At the very least, it was easy. It made him think of living alone, about not being able to do the simplest tasks yourself. What would this woman do were she to fall down a flight of stairs? She would lie there, alone.

Just as he had seen the webs as a civilization when he first walked up, now it was as though he were a god, coming with a cataclysm. This cataclysm was in the form of a long black plastic tube that sucked up the webs and the spiders and the spiders' caches of bug meat with great force. He found a stepladder in the open garage as well, and to finish the work he stood on it and got the highest corners; where the oldest, grubbiest webbing was, there was a white gluey paste. So old even the spiders didn't go there anymore.

When the woman returned fifteen minutes later, he'd already put the Shop-Vac and broom and ladder away. She looked at him from the driveway, still seated in her large brown Pontiac, and Matt heard the thoomp-pop of the trunk, and the woman said, "Will you get that bag outta there for me?"

"Ma'am?"

"I'm not playing any tricks on you," she said. "I'll tell you where Mary is. I can't carry the damned thing. I only went to get it because you were here. Otherwise it would sit and rot in the trunk for a month." She smiled.

"I really would like to know," he said, standing in her backyard with the thirty-pound bag in his arms. "I promise you I'm not pretending."

"Mary left Sturgeon Bay about three years ago," said the woman. "Tear that open."

Matt lowered the bag to the ground and ripped at the corner of the plastic. As he did this, the woman went on. "To tell you the honest truth, I don't know where she went. She was a strange girl."

"But you do strange."

"I do strange."

"Strange how?"

"Restless."

"Did you ever know her sister?"

"Which one?"

Matt remembered that she was only Caroline's half sister. "How many has she got?"

"I don't know," said the woman. "Thirty. Forty."

"That's a joke, I assume."

"I never laugh when I make my own jokes," said the woman. "To me that's ridiculous."

"Her name's Caroline," he said. "For a time her name was Caroline Francis. I'm not sure what it is now."

The woman, hands on her hips, nodded to a bird feeder hanging on a low branch of a maple tree. "No. Never knew her. Mary didn't have many people showing up as visitors."

Matt raised the bag and started pouring the seed. He watched the black and white and yellow seed fill in the box behind a wall of plastic. "Do you know anyone who knows where Mary Landower might be?"

The woman nodded. "I do. But do you know anything about plumbing?"

4

If Matt went way way way way back, he could remember things. Not a lot. There was nothing before the age of five. After five, there was the first foster family, the Marcams. That far back, he'd been so young that he didn't know any better than to accept whatever happened as the same thing that happened to everybody. And the Marcams had given him no real reason to doubt it, at least in the beginning. They were rich. He couldn't remember the whole story, but later, after they'd already sent him back, another boy told him that Mrs. Marcam couldn't get pregnant, and that's why she came in and tried new kids on for size so often. The man had almost never been home. He was thin and fit and austere and had rarely spoken to Matt. Mrs. Marcam, though, had taken him everywhere, had never left his side. He'd gone shopping with her and gone to the YMCA with her and accompanied the Marcams on vacations — there was a beach, even, and he could remember running across it, in the sand, and holding on to a flat stone he'd found, running back with it to show her. There was one trip into the mountains, too, somewhere out west, and Matt remembered sitting on her lap on a balcony and looking out on snowcapped peaks and her leaning over him and saying, "This is what beautiful is." She wore strong perfume. Once, Marissa had come home wearing something similar, and he'd gotten a little weak in the knees and said, "What perfume is that?" without looking at her, and she said it was something she'd gotten at the department store, a sample. He asked her if she'd bought it and she said no, so he didn't say anything else. If she'd bought it, then he would have asked her never to wear it.

What went wrong was simple. It was maybe a year after he'd arrived. He came home with a hole in the knee of his pants after playing with two neighborhood boys and falling on their driveway and skinning his knee. The skin was raw and bloody when he walked in and she'd run over, hands up in the air, and had examined it carefully. Then, as she was putting the Band-Aids on him, after she'd washed it, she just started to cry. Then, very quietly, she'd said, "You haven't the faintest idea how much these pants cost me, do you, you little asshole?"

A week later he was back at the boys' home.

There were not many more chores. Two hours' worth. Matt helped her with a clog in her bathtub, and then, after some cajoling, he mowed her lawn. He drew the line at going to Wal-Mart with her to "get some things."

He did, though, get information. The woman who had known Mary well had moved to Green Bay. He got the address and drove straight down, once released. His whole idea of the quick in and quick out was already fading away; it was well into the afternoon, and Matt was beginning to doubt he'd return home tonight with anything. He drove with one hand on the wheel, no radio, and accepted the end of the quick recovery.

He didn't know what had made him think of Mrs. Marcam. Maybe something about the old woman in Sturgeon Bay, or maybe a question: where was Mrs. Marcam now, and was she an old woman, and was she being taken care of by her husband, or somebody? Or was she taking care of someone else? Had she found any children or settled on a particular group? Or still, to this day, was she rotating them like pets? Loneliness, maybe. Loneliness always made him think of her.

Green Bay came up on him quickly, and he had to stop and ask directions twice to find the right area. When he did, he saw the big house was just off Mason Street. It looked a hundred years old at least. It was orange and black, coated with broad wooden shingles that looked like fish scales. There was a spire shooting up from the roof, out of the third floor. At the front was a porch and a long driveway that led into the old Queen Anne house's back lot. The whole structure looked to be in disrepair; Matt didn't know whether or not it was an illusion, but when he looked at the spire his mind told him the angle was slightly off, that it wasn't quite plumb, that it was leaning like an old tree. Even from where he stood at the front of the driveway, he could see the foundation was a disaster. He would not have been particularly surprised to see the whole damned thing rumble a bit, then sink down into the maw of the earth amid a cloud of smoke.

He went to the front porch and climbed the stairs. There was a doorbell, but when he pressed it he had the distinct impression absolutely nothing was happening within the bowels of the house's electrical system.

He knocked loudly.

He waited for about a minute, then knocked again.

Finally, as the very beginnings of relief and plans of returning home were edging toward the front of his mind, and the very idea of releasing the cradle and the Civil War was strengthening, he heard the sounds of metal sliding. Once, twice, then a third time. The great door swung open, into the house.

An ancient woman stood before him. Below him, actually. She was four feet tall.

"Oh," she said. "Hello, young man."

Like the house, she could not have been younger than one hundred years old. Her hair was stark white, puffed and sticking out in every direction. In her withered, rheumatic hand Matt saw a cigarette burning. A blue dress clung tenuously to her skeletal frame. She was barefoot. Curled yellow toenails stretched away from each toe.

"Hello, ma'am," Matt said, looking down at her.

He thought to go to one knee for the conversation but reconsidered, and instead just took off his hat. "I was wondering if I could have a minute of your time."

"You certainly can," the woman said. "I'm having fun already."

"I was just up in Door County," he said, and he pointed his thumb over his shoulder, toward the driveway. "I was speaking to a woman there named Hannah Price."

"Oh," said the woman. A smile lit up her face. Matt saw the ash on the cigarette drop down and land on top of the woman's foot. She didn't seem to notice. "Hannah. What a nice young girl. Yes. Lovely."

"I'm looking for someone named Mary Landower. Hannah told me you might know where she is."

"I do, certainly," said the woman. "Mary Landower lives in Antarctica."

Matt nodded. "Yes," he said. "Okay."

"Would you like to come in?" she asked. "Would you like some tea? You look tired, young man. Why don't you come in? Why are you looking for Mary? And how was Hannah? Did she look happy?"

Inside the old house, Matt sat at the table, watching the old woman as she moved about the kitchen. She'd already stubbed out the first unsmoked cigarette, and another was stuffed into the gap between her fingers, burning. He'd yet to see her actually touch a cigarette to her lips. Lost ash littered the linoleum floor. The kettle was on, and a pot was ready and waiting on the countertop. The woman, whose name was Sylvia (Ancient Sylvia, Matt's mind said, and after he heard it once in his brain, he had trouble not thinking it over and over again), had settled into an easy chatter as though she'd known him for twenty years. "Now I don't think you could technically call it science, what she's doing. And don't ask me how she got them to take her there. She's persistent, I suppose."

Ancient Sylvia used to have a house in Sturgeon Bay, she'd explained, and from time to time, Mary had stopped in to check up on her. Her house had been only a few doors down.

"Did you ever know her sister?"

"No," said the woman, pausing at the sink for a moment. "I never knew anyone in her life."

"Why'd she come to see you all the time?"

"I suppose because I was so old!"

Matt thought about agreeing with the woman about her age but then thought it might be rude. The water began to boil, and Matt watched as Sylvia shuffled toward it. He saw her trying to lift the heavy kettle with the same hand that held the cigarette — ash now spilled down onto her wrist and into the stovetop — and he stood and said, "I can do that," and poured the hot water into the teapot.

"Thank you very much," she said.

The tea steeped, and Matt sat back down.

"Why do you need Mary now?" she asked him. "Is she your lover?"

"Not in the least."

"I see. What, then?"

"Her sister," Matt said, "is my mother-in-law. Not that I've ever met her. But I'm looking for her because she's got something I need."

"What has she got?"

"A cradle," he said. "For a baby."

Ancient Sylvia's face collapsed and reconstituted itself into a beaming smile.

"So you must be having a baby," she said.

"I am," he said. "My wife is, I mean. I'm just observing."

She brought the teapot to the table, then went back to the cupboard for the cups. In between the cups and the milk and the sugar, she lit another cigarette. "I love babies," she said, sitting down. "I have one."

Matt, in the middle of pouring her tea, looked up at her.

"Had," she said, nodding a little, looking past him to the wall. "Had." She turned her old blue eyes to him. "He's not a baby anymore, of course. Now he's a troll."

Matt poured his own tea.

"Milk, ma'am?" he said to her.

"Thank you." Her cigarette was now entirely one long tube of ash. It was no longer even burning. "My advice to you about children," she said, "is to make sure they leave eventually. They have an amazing habit of coming back, over and over again. Keep them close to your heart early on. Then make them leave."

"Does that mean yours hasn't?"

"My troll lives upstairs in the attic."

Matt looked up at the ceiling.

"We'll need him," she said, "if we want to call Mary. We'll need his special skills. Do you want to call Mary?"

"Call her?" he asked. "We can call her?"

"Yes, of course," she said. "Do you not know about the Internet?"

"I know about it."

"You see, all the computers in the world are now hooked together into one large computer," said the woman.

"Yes," Matt said. "I know that."

"And by using them together, they can talk to one another, and you can control them."

"I know that."

"Let me call Brian," she said. "Hold on."

As the woman stood, Matt again had to push away the notion that his job was finished. Since the tea began he'd been thinking about the drive home, calculating times. Would there be traffic in Milwaukee for the ride home? What speed would he set his cruise to? Now, again, it seemed as though there were a glimmer of hope. Which was the exact opposite of what he wanted. Once it was extinguished, he could go, but the flame wasn't out yet. It was still burning and Marissa back home was still upright in the chair, envisioning the cradle coming back. Ancient Sylvia was at a bank of drawers now, near the sink. She pulled one open and rifled through it. She said, "Ah," then withdrew a black object and turned to show him. "Walkie-talkie," she said. It was an older model, the type that kids had played with when Matt was growing up, with a long rubber antenna and orange buttons on the front. The woman twisted some knobs, and the sound of static filled the room.

She ashed her cigarette on the floor, then moved the walkie-talkie to her mouth, pressed the button down, and said, "Brian, if you don't mind, we'd like to use the computer. Over." This last word she added with a touch of glee.

She released and there was more static.

"I'm busy, Mother. Over."

It was a man's voice, lost in the back of a cave.

"I have company," Ancient Sylvia said. "We need to use it. I'm sure whatever you're doing can wait. Over."

"It can't. Over."

"Brian," said Ancient Sylvia in a more authoritative voice.

There was a long pause of static.

Ancient Sylvia waited, staring down at the walkie-talkie.

"Fine. Come up."

She smiled again. "There, you see?" she said to Matt, turning and putting the walkie-talkie back into the drawer. "Let's go upstairs."

The old woman rambled her way out of the kitchen, her bare feet padding on the linoleum, then into the next room and over the carpet. This room had four couches in it, all of them different colors. The walls were yellow-white. She moved very slowly, and Matt went very slowly behind her. He could see the beginning of a staircase at the far side of the room. He took one step, then stopped. She took three. Leaning against the wall near a grandfather clock was a cane, and the old woman made a detour to get it. Finally, they reached the bottom of the stairs.

"Here we are," she said, looking at him over her shoulder. "Now we start to go up. These stairs will take us to the next floor."

He nodded.

"And then again."

He nodded.

She turned back and started to climb.

Fifteen minutes later they'd reached the third floor of the house.

They were in another den, this one far more minimal. An open door led off to a bedroom, and Matt saw more stairs in the far corner. These were spiral, and went up into a hole in the ceiling. He assumed it was the spire he'd seen from the outside.

"Since Brian knows we're coming, this shouldn't be a problem," said Sylvia, who reached into her dress pocket and pulled out another cigarette. Slowly she lit it, and Matt waited to see if she would take a drag. Instead she said, "Do you like them?"

"Like what?"

"The pockets," she said. She pointed down and then tapped the pockets on her dress. They were a different color than the fabric, Matt saw. "I sewed them in," she said.

"They're nice."

"It was not difficult," she said. "And I decided there was no good reason to not have pockets. Men have pockets, always. Look at you. You have pockets."

Matt looked down at his pockets.

"Now I have them, too, you see," she said.

They made their way to the next staircase. Then, slowly, they started winding up. The old woman took even longer climbing these stairs, as they were steeper and required a slight twist of the body. He resisted the impulse to pick her up by the armpits and carry her the rest of the way.

Once his head had gone over the level of the ceiling, he could see anyway, so he spent the last minutes of the climb taking in the room. Computers. There were eight computer screens in this room, arranged on a circular desk that wrapped all the way around its interior. There were cables everywhere — power strips overflowing with other power strips, black and yellow and red and white cords snaking along the walls, where they'd been stapled sloppily in place. Matt thought he could smell something rancid in the air, too, like a wet dog's bed left to mold. There were windows all around the circular room, higher than only the cords and the desk. There was a small platform around the stairwell where one could stand. The rest of the space was taken up by Brian.

Brian.

He was a troll. The old woman was right. The man's long, thin back, hunched, was essentially all Matt could see, save the bald crown of his head and the ring of dark, greasy hair that hung down past the T-shirt's collar. The spine stuck up and ran down the center of the shirt. The skin was inhumanly pale.

"Brian is writing a book," said the old woman, once they'd both arrived at the landing. "It's about history."

Finally the man turned to look. His face was softer than Matt had expected. What had he expected? The face of a monster? At the very least sharp, angry features. This man looked sad, and his face drooped. His eyes were bloodshot. He looked tired. He looked at least sixty. The top of his head was sweaty — this was not surprising, as it was twenty degrees hotter in this room than in any of the others.

PATRICK SOMERVILLE

"Hello," he said loudly, as though he were calling to Matt across a great distance.

"Hello," Matt said, trying to give him an example of a better volume.

"He needs to speak with Mary Landower in Antarctica," said Ancient Sylvia, also loudly. She leaned toward him and said more quietly, "Using the *Internet*."

"All right, Ma," said Brian, swiveling back in front of his computer monitor. "I know. You said it on the walkie-talkie anyway."

He pointed to another monitor, and Matt saw a small stool beneath the desk. "She might be there."

Matt sat down.

"Oh, she'll be there," said Ancient Sylvia. "Where else does she have to go?"

"I don't know," said Brian. "How about a crevasse somewhere?"

"Crev-what?"

"She might be somewhere," Brian said. He looked at Matt. "She might be somewhere. It's not like this is *Star Trek*."

He turned back to his monitor and clicked a few times. Matt watched him moving boxes around on the screen. He knew nothing about computers and only barely knew what the Internet was himself. Not because he'd never had a chance to learn but because he'd avoided it on purpose.

"She's there," Brian said. "Hold on."

A few more clicks, and a window opened up on the monitor in front of Matt. In the window, for an instant, there was a man, poorly shaven, wearing an old gray hat. Then Matt realized it was his own picture.

He leaned forward, and the picture of himself leaned forward as well.

"So this is video, then?" he said.

"No," said Brian. "I just happened to do, like, totally perfect CGI animation last night and it just happens to look exactly like you."

"Brian," scolded Ancient Sylvia. "Sass."

Brian ignored her. "You should appreciate this. Do you know how amazing this is? This is nineteen ninety-seven. You are dealing with two thousand three technology here, my friend. She has it down there because of the government. I have it up here because I am a master of the universe."

Another box opened up in front of Matt then. The picture, at first, was a number of small colored boxes blinking in and out, and only after several seconds did the boxes start to meld together into somebody's face. Once the video settled, he saw the woman. She was squinting, and behind her he could see the blinking lights of other computers and machinery. She was wearing a bright red cap; her face was thin and angular, and she had a certain cold beauty to her. Matt thought of her as an Ice Queen, sitting high atop her throne in a faraway castle. Something flapped over her right shoulder.

"Hello, Syl," she was saying, but then she frowned. She appeared to be looking away from the camera. Then Matt realized she was looking at his picture on her end. "Who's that?"

"Hello?" Matt said.

He looked at Brian, who nodded sarcastically.

"Hello, Mrs. Landower?"

"Yes?"

"My name is Matt Bishop," he said. "I'm sitting here at Sylvia's house. I came here to ask her a question."

"You seem to be talking to me!" The woman was yelling.

Matt realized now the wind was blowing on her end, and the wall behind her was rattling.

"Well, the question —"

"We have a storm coming!"

"The question —"

"Does this have something to do with me?"

"It does," Matt said. He found himself starting to talk louder, too. "My wife — my wife is the daughter of your sister Caroline."

The woman sat quietly for a moment on the other end of the line — her eyes ticked up and went to the camera, which made it seem as though she were looking directly into his eyes.

The picture flickered for a moment. Then she said, "Marissa?"

"Yes."

She nodded. Someone walked past then, behind her. Matt saw only a man's torso, hurrying somewhere. Mary yelled, "Caroline has always had a problem with . . . staying in one place!"

"So she's alive."

"Yes," yelled Mary. "She's alive!" There was a loud bang, and Mary looked over her shoulder.

"Where can I find her?" Matt said.

"What?"

"Where can I find her?"

"You can't. She's too far away."

"How far away?"

"She's . . . do . . . nesia."

"What?"

"Indonesia!"

"I'm looking for a cradle," Matt said.

"A what?"

"A cradle!"

"A cradle?"

"For Marissa! It's — we're having a baby!"

"Is it something she used to have?"

"Yes!"

"Everything that…her…Darren…sota!"

"What?"

"Everything that she…with Darren in Minnesota."

"Darren?"

"Yes! Her husband!"

"In Minnesota?"

"Yes!…Anything…take…that sonofabitch!"

"Do you have an address?"

"Hold on!"

She disappeared. Matt looked over at Brian, who had stopped paying attention. Ancient Sylvia, behind him, was rapt. She nodded her encouragement to him. "You seem to be doing quite well," she said. "If I speak to her for too long, she often switches to different languages."

Mary came back on the screen, now holding something in her lap and looking down at it. "If you go to find him," she yelled, "do me a favor!"

"Okay," Matt said.

"Tell him Mary says he's an asshole!"

Matt was halfway across Wisconsin before the night caught up with him and he decided he needed to sleep. He had a long way to go, and he wasn't going to be getting anywhere near Walton, Minnesota, anytime soon. He didn't want to go all night. A few miles after he decided, he came upon a rest stop. He pulled the truck in, found a distant parking spot, killed the engine, leaned his head back, and put his hat down, arms crossed. After a few minutes he opened his eyes. He opened the glove compartment and removed one Twinkie, unwrapped it, and ate it slowly. He looked at the *Gazetteer*, a dark shape on the seat beside him, then looked toward the bathrooms and saw a pay phone and thought of calling Marissa. She would know, however, that he was still looking. She wouldn't be worried about him. He could call and say, "I'd like to come back now." No. Through the windshield, in the distance, he could see the bright white glow of a light hanging above the bathrooms. Far away, there were a few other cars around and the cab of a semitruck. A woman, a lone hooker maybe, leaned against the cab of the truck and talked up to the window. Even at this distance, he could see the black spots of insects crowded around the huge light above it all. Thousands of them.

5

It was February. Adam had been gone for six weeks and he was there, on the ground.

She didn't know what he did day to day. Bill knew. As far as dealing with information went, she saw two paths — on one, she was demanding news, always, as though seeking some kind of omniscience or overhead view of the battlefields and the cities. She was scouring the Internet for articles and spending time looking at maps. She was trying to know everything.

On the other, she was disconnected and blank.

For the first month she'd chosen the godlike path and tried to look down from above. She read the news daily and chatted online with other mothers of soldiers late at night, did almost nothing with her long days, slept late. Wrote little.

Now she'd gone to the other edge. Now she exercised, ate well, enjoyed Adam's calls when they came, and with all her other time pretended there was no such thing as war. If he was in danger, Adam never told her. They talked about his friends, the weather, and the football games the soldiers played. For all she knew, he was either playing catch or napping on a cot somewhere, always. This is how she thought of him and this is how she planned to think of him until he came home. There was no other way she could deal with it.

"Your pills," Bill said, his toast in hand. "You have your sleeping pills?"

"I do," she said. She'd decided not to bring the whole bottle and had simply shaken six of the tablets into a baggie for the flights. No need to be tempted to sleep the entire vacation away.

The doctor had told her two would knock her out for the duration of the flight. She planned on taking three. Bill didn't know this and she wasn't going to tell him. He would be concerned, but he had always been afraid of doctors and what they advised. She was not that way. She was the kind of person who altered doctors' suggestions when it seemed like the right idea.

What she wanted from the pills was this: they'd drive to O'Hare, park, move through security, read the newspaper, and board the plane. She would close her eyes as the engines warmed up, there would be a darkness, a lifting feeling, and when she opened her eyes, it would be nine hours later, and they would be in beautiful Hawaii.

Bill had convinced her the trip really was, after all, a good idea. A week on the beach, bright sun, far away from the depressing muck landscape of the dark Midwest.

"There is nothing more deadly," Bill liked to say, "than February in Illinois."

And there was something to this, she had to admit. She had been thinking of all the green they would see. Even though there were more deadly things.

Bill held out the second piece of toast toward her. "Do you want it?" he said.

The first part of her plan went as scripted, and she waited until they were seated at the gate before digging into her purse and finding the pills. The doctor said about twenty minutes after she took them. She looked at the screen to be sure there would be no delays; everything appeared to be right. The two gate clerks in their red vests and white blouses tapped busily and happily on their keyboards as though they were Muppets, and behind them, the red dotted lights of the board spelled out HONOLULU, 12:15. As Renee watched, one of the Muppet clerks picked up the black phone and announced they would begin boarding in only a few moments.

"I'm going to take the pills now, I think," she said to Bill.

Bill glanced up from the paper. "Don't you want to wait until we get on the plane?"

"I want as little plane as possible," she said. "We're going now anyway." Bill looked up and watched the people milling about in a quasi-line chunk. "They take a few minutes to kick in."

"All right," he said, shrugging. "Whatever." He folded his paper. "If we have to make an emergency landing, I'll do my best to drag you into a raft."

"Don't joke."

"Not a joke," he said.

She spotted a water fountain across the wide concourse and stood. The airport was not busy, something that seemed almost impossible for Chicago. Most of the gates were sparse; there were seats everywhere. She saw a family all sitting together in a circle at a nearly empty gate. They were playing UNO.

Across the concourse hallway, she placed one pill on her tongue and sipped the water. What dreams will I have? she wondered. Probably none at all. Probably a black curtain. The last time she had taken sleeping pills, it had been just as she hoped it would be. A big fuzzy God hand reaching down out of the sky, taking hold of a lever in her mind, pushing it down into the TOTAL SHUTDOWN position, some more severe setting than even SLEEP. FALSE DEATH, she thought. Whatever it was that Juliet had, whatever fake poison that had been. That's what she wanted now. When I wake up, she thought, I will be somewhere else. I will be almost as far away as Adam.

She looked over her shoulder at Bill, still seated across the way, waiting patiently, watching her, legs crossed.

She smiled at him, then found herself waving. No reason. He gave a funny smile back, shook his head, and waved as well. His wave plus his funny smile said: why are we waving across the concourse at the airport?

She turned to the water and took two more pills. She thought of the sun, and of Hawaii, of being somewhere else. The baggie was still in her hand. She reached into it and pulled out one more with the tip of her finger. It stuck there, and she held it up, then placed it on her tongue. Just to be sure.

Renee had been in love two times in her life and had slept with only two men. The loves were very different — one winter, one summer. Had Jonathan not been killed, it would have been only one love and one man, and her heart would be impressed with only one imprint. Her landscape would be something easy and traversable — she would be something like a flat prairie, like the farmland in Wisconsin.

She sometimes wondered: would I be simple, then, if he lived? She thought of her heart as a fractured and complex thing, some cratered mass of treacherous slopes and sinkholes, not at all something simple and easy. On the far side there was the flat prairie, the original open place, that was Jonathan. On the other side, past the enormous divide, there was the luxury hotel that was Bill, safe and stable, even though on that end it was always winter. The in-between landscape was the shattered land.

She thought of the burning factory she'd seen on television with Bill that night. It was the perfect kind of structure for this in-between: it was just what you'd come to as you were making the journey from one to the next. That first love was so long ago, thousands and thousands of years, and yet he was still there in her mind, she still knew him, she still felt him. One night she'd been drifting off to sleep and she heard him yell her name from downstairs; her head shot up, and Bill looked at her, and she said, Oh, it's nothing, and then went into the bathroom and cried. She saw him all the time. There he was, for example, at the Foster Avenue Beach in 1968, dripping as he came up out of the water in his blue trunks, coming to lie down beside her in the sun, his dark hair flattened down on his head, his lean muscles tan. He was so young. Adam's age. Was that possible? The two long blue veins running up each of his forearms, meeting together at the underside of his elbows. And they reappeared along the biceps and ran up along the fronts of his shoulders and disappeared as they snaked beneath the skin and flesh of his chest. That image, the image of him walking toward her, was both false and true. It had happened over and over again for one entire summer, so who could say whether her mind made it by piecing all the perfect parts together? It didn't matter. Besides, it was only the entryway into her thinking. That picture was the first page of Jonathan. On the last page he was lying alone in a jungle, half gone.

They met at a party. She was a freshman at Northwestern, he was someone's cousin. He had not been bothered about knowing no one, about not being a student. She remembered closing her eyes and leaning against a table and swaying back and forth to the strange music filling the house. It was foreign and had scales she didn't know and a drumbeat with no changes, just pounding, da da da da da da da da da da da da da da daa. When she opened her eyes, she saw him across the room. He was holding a joint and talking to someone, speaking emphatically, moving his right hand up and down to illustrate his points even as he moved the joint slowly to his lips. Stoned, and high on some pill she'd taken with a girl in the bathroom, she found herself staring at him for what felt like five minutes. Whatever part of her brain that kept telling her not to look at someone forever had either stopped working or made a special exception for this person.

Finally he saw her looking. How could he not? When he crossed the room and approached her, she stood up straight.

She felt as if her eyes were barely open.

He said, "Hi. You look like you're about to die."

The music was loud, and he had to lean close to her. Even then, it was a yell.

"I just can't understand what this *music* is," she yelled. "It's so funny."

"What's your name?"

"I'm Renee," she yelled. "That is my friend Steven over there," she yelled, nodding in one direction, "and that is my friend Sheila over there," she yelled, nodding in another. "What are you?"

"What am I?"

"I mean, who are we?" she yelled.

"Who are we?" he asked. "I guess you're Renee and I'm Jonathan. Hi."

She introduced herself to him again.

"You already introduced yourself," he yelled. "I'm Jonathan. Hi. Honestly, are you okay?"

"I'm fine, Jonathan," she said, tilting her head. "I was just looking at you. Did you see me looking at you?"

"That's why I came over here."

"Do you want to know what I was thinking while I was looking at you?"

"What?" he yelled back.

"I SAID, DO YOU WANT TO KNOW WHAT I WAS THINKING WHILE I WAS LOOKING AT YOU?" she yelled.

"Yes," he said, nodding. "I do."

"I WAS THINKING," she yelled, "THAT YOU LOOK LIKE A PRINCE."

"A prince?" he yelled. "That's nice. I actually think my family comes from peasants."

"No, no, no, no, no," she said, shaking her head, smiling at him. She slapped him on the shoulder. "You glow," she said. She looked up at the ceiling then, thinking. When she looked back at him, she said, "I know exactly who you are."

"Who am I?" he said.

"Why?" she said.

"Uhhh," he said. "I don't know?"

"Who are you?"

"I don't go to your school. I'm just here, living with my uncle and my cousin —"

"You are Charles Martel."

Jonathan stopped talking, leaned back, and stood up straight. "Thank you very much, Renee." Someone was dancing right behind him, she saw, a blond-haired girl. She was shaking her head. Another student was nearby, a boy she knew from class, and she looked at him and looked at his mouth moving and could see by the way his mouth moved that he said the words *Tet Offensive*. It was sometime near the beginning of 1968, cold outside but unbearably hot in this apartment. The music was loud. She turned away from the student and looked again at this Jonathan.

"I don't feel tired, Bill," Renee said.

"They probably just haven't kicked in yet."

"It's been forty-five minutes," she said. "And I feel awake." It didn't feel like the fuzzy God hand had reached down and turned her brain off. Actually, it felt like she'd been struck by lightning.

"Very awake," she said.

"Where are the pills?"

"What?"

"Where are your sleeping pills?"

"In my bag," she said. She reached down for her purse and began digging for the baggie. "I just brought a few."

"Let me see them."

She found the baggie, looked at it, and handed it over to him. He adjusted the overhead light and squinted at the midsize yellow capsules. He held them close to his nose.

"Problem," he said.

"What?" she said.

"These aren't sleeping pills," he said.

"What are they?"

"These are Adam's," he said, twisting his wrist to show her.

"These are the ADHD pills." He glanced at her. "You just took amphetamines, dear."

"That's not possible," she said, snatching the bag. "I just — he stopped taking those two years ago." She stared at the capsules. There it was, in tiny white writing.

ADDERALL

"We still had a bottle in the cabinet," Bill said. "The refill? It was still there. He quit and we kept them because we didn't know if he'd want to start again."

"Oh dear."

"You must have picked up the wrong one this morning."

Renee stared straight ahead at the back of the seat in front of her. Bill was smiling. "Look, you'll be fine. You'll just be a little focused for a while. You took two, right? It'll wear off in a couple of hours. Read your book."

She turned to him. "I took four."

"*Four?*" he asked loudly. He looked around and then said, more quietly, "Why in God's name would you take four?"

"Because I wanted to sleep well."

"Are you trying to overdose?"

"If I wanted to overdose, I'd take thirty."

"I'm thrilled you have a plan for that."

"It's not a plan," she said, stuffing the baggie back into her purse. "It's logic. I'm telling you, this was an accident anyway."

"Okay, okay," Bill said, hands up. "Let's get you some water." He pressed the overhead button for the stewardess and said, "I'm wondering if this is the kind of problem that makes them turn the plane around."

"I'll be fine. So it's some speed. I existed in the seventies."

"You were maybe not so on edge in the seventies."

71

"Just stop," she said. "Stop, Bill. Okay? I'm fine. I'll write."

She had a notebook. She'd stuffed it into her purse this morning. She'd thought that maybe, given the right feeling — the right evening on the beach, the right wind coming from the water — her mind would turn back to the last white note card on the board and show her some way to write it.

It had persisted in the back of her mind these last months. She'd done nothing. She'd been thinking of Adam, and the poems had, in the last months, begun to feel embarrassing. Never mind whether or not they were good — embarrassing because she'd written them at all, because she had become a middle-aged woman writing poems in her study. It was something she should have been proud of. A younger version of herself would have been proud. Now it looked capricious and escapist, glibly bourgeoisie, some silly grab at self-therapy, not art, not anything that mattered.

And yet the board had stayed up. The blank note card was still there. She had begun to believe that finishing it would finish everything. Write the poem, and the feeling will be out of you, there will be something complete. Everyone can move on. You will never have to think of it again. If that formula was true, then it was so close, only ten lines away, and she would have her freedom. They got the water and Bill rubbed her neck a bit and asked her how she felt. The answer was, she felt her heart beating in her chest and was aware of every artery, vein, and capillary that snaked through the skin of her face, her neck, and along the sides of her head. The round muscles at the bottom of her jaw were twitching. Already she had a headache. She said she felt fine, like she'd had too much coffee. Bill seemed skeptical, but he turned back to his newspaper. She closed her eyes, pen in hand, not knowing what she would write. She listened to the sound of the engine and she found herself there with Jonathan on some airplane as well, crossing the ocean, and then there with him as he landed.

What was it? Hot. Humid. His letters — there were only four letters — had said that the humidity was what he couldn't get over, and that he walked off the plane and it was like walking into water. And so she imagined him in all the places she could think to imagine him — sitting near a stream, gun resting across his legs. Sleeping in a barracks. Pacing through the jungle, crouched low, forming one arm of a triangle of other men doing the same. It was everything she'd gotten from movies.

She wrote this. First she just listed the images that came into her mind, but she found herself, after filling a page with the images, connecting them to one another, trying to make a story out of it. She made Jonathan thinking of her at night but doing his best to not think of her at other times because thinking of her would distract him, and being distracted would get him killed. Then he was in Saigon, sitting at an outdoor café, writing a letter to her. Around him the city was alive and moving. She didn't know what details to fill it with, so she just tried to think of people. An old man walking slowly. A prostitute yelling at another table of soldiers. Children. Palm trees? She didn't know. She took these images and did her best to weave them in with what she had written about him in the jungle. She found herself writing whole paragraphs about things she didn't know about, things like what Jonathan thought of his aunt and uncle in Chicago; what Jonathan thought, truly, about the war; what Jonathan planned to do when he returned. She found herself writing one of his thoughts: he didn't know whether he would marry her. It hurt to write it. She wondered whether it was true. He had promised her he would and she had believed him, absolutely. "I understand the right thing to do," he'd said. But. What if she had spent the better part of her life thinking of what could have been between them and he had died there, unsure whether he loved her? Whether he was trapped? Was such a thing possible? She never wrote to him about herself, back home in Chicago. She never mentioned the classes, sitting at desks, taking notes, explaining to her parents that they had not given him enough of a chance, and that when he came home, they'd know him, really know him, and she and he would be married and they would appreciate him.

It broke down before she could bring herself to write the scene of his death. She had thought about it, of course. She had wondered. In the first days she knew only "killed in combat." Then she became obsessed, she wanted to know the exact details. She had made phone call after phone call to any military office she could find, but those calls had been only frustrating and had gone nowhere. Later she waited for a letter to arrive from somebody Jonathan knew, somebody who'd been with him. Others had to have been there. She convinced herself that one day she'd walk to the mailbox and find a spare, simple note telling her what had happened, what they'd tried to do to help him, why it hadn't worked, and what Jonathan had been saying. Some soldier friend of his would have taken it upon himself to seek her out and write the note and let her know. Instead his body arrived and they were not allowed to open the casket because he'd been incinerated.

His parents came to Chicago for the funeral. Renee wrote about them — how his mother cried and how she wanted to talk to her about Jonathan and how Renee found herself unable to give the woman what she wanted, and by the end had just walked away from her. How the big father hadn't said a word the entire time. She wrote about his beard and his gray hair, his immense body — nothing like Jonathan's — his suspenders, the passive sadness in his eyes as he sipped water at the wake and nodded to people. How uncomfortable he was in Chicago. How out of place he felt in their home. She couldn't remember his first name. She waited, pen poised on paper, for it to come, but it didn't.

It was as though, then, her heart had exhausted itself of Jonathan and moved on to the middle ground, the broken landscape. What she scribbled sounded like a children's story. The tone was altered now, all those stories she'd written, all the ways of making the language simple, making it so any mind could come to it and read it. A transparency but something warm, and then much farther down, something complicated. That was always what she had wanted. She thought of a boy — a boy-prince but someone new, not the happily wry Thomas from her book but someone darker, older, angrier, silent, and she was writing scenes of him traveling across this broken landscape, trying to get from one place to the next, from A to B to Z. Some quest. He would meet with other travelers and speak with them and move on. She didn't bother filling in what he was seeking, as that didn't matter in any story — instead she wrote about him alone in the mountains and then down in the valleys, always moving forward, always intent on his path, but far above she was looking down at him, and she could see how impossible it was for him to reach his destination. Terrible, terrible things happened to him as he went, but she brushed over them and didn't let herself show them completely. She couldn't. From that high above, she could see that this distance he had to go was impossible. But he didn't know it. She did not allow him to ever get up high enough to see how arduous the journey was, because had he known, there was a chance that he would have stopped. He had to not know in order to continue.

For hours this went on. She was not well. Her eyes felt twitchy. Bill would check with her and she would say she was okay. Fine. He would look at the notebook, watch as her hand moved the pen and filled page after page. She would wait for him to ask what she was writing, but he never did. Instead he read. A little later he went to sleep.

She kept writing, her hand sore. Her stomach was tight but she wasn't hungry, she couldn't imagine eating. Her mind was a straight tunnel and there was only one clear circle of light ahead. She stayed with it and refused to leave it and kept writing, even as the words made less sense, as she abandoned sentences altogether for an hour. The letters of her script began to sag and angle. Her handwriting was falling apart. She was not tired, not in the least, when she leaned over toward Bill's sleeping face and looked out the window and down and saw that, far below them, what seemed like miles down, all you could see was the ocean. Still she wasn't through. She went back to who she had been in the weeks after the funeral, still going to class, still reading. She moved back to her parents' home, then blank. She wrote about the long month of December, and Christmas. Her father gave her the Whitman book that year. She would not be going back for the spring semester, but he wanted her to have something to read and think about while they waited. "Your imagination should be working," her father had said. "Whatever happens in there also happens in there." One point to the head, one point to the belly.

They were on the ground. The notebook was nearly full. She packed it away into her purse. Bill asked her if she was all right and she said fine and he asked her again at the luggage terminal and she said fine again.

Someone gave them leis. It was remarkably humid here, too.

She couldn't help but notice it as she stood beside her husband on the sidewalk and waited for a cab to pull up. "What time is it?" she asked Bill. "It's two o'clock," he said. She thought of telling him to take off his lei, that it made him ridiculous. "It's like we've been going back in time," she said instead. "The way the time zones work." As they waited, a woman beside her smoked a cigarette and talked on the phone. "I don't know and you don't know," the woman said. "He don't know neither. That makes several of us." Renee looked at the woman intently. She was squat and fat, with dark brown hair. She was Hawaiian. She was wearing a white tank top and she held the phone to her ear with her right hand and moved the cigarette away from her lips with her left. She had a tattoo on her left shoulder, and when she turned and saw Renee watching her, she smiled.

The cab came. They loaded the luggage in. Bill asked if she was okay and she said that she was but that she wanted to lie down. She felt sick when they started moving and she opened the window and closed her eyes, letting the humid air flow over her face. She didn't open her eyes, and at the hotel, Bill got into an argument with the man behind the desk, slick-haired and young and obnoxiously professional. "Do you see, right here, my confirmation number?" she heard Bill asking, holding a slip of paper up. "No smoking," he said. "My wife is sick. We'd like to have our room. Our room that doesn't stink like smoke." "I assure you, sir, it will not smell like smoke in your room. For tonight, I can put you there, and if there are any problems, we'll move you first thing in the morning." "This is unacceptable." "I'm very sorry, sir, but it's all I can do right now. We have the Pro Bowl." "You have got to be kidding me." "No, sir." "What is a reservation for then, exactly? I'm curious for future reference." "There were some extenuating circumstances this year, sir. You see, there was a miscommunication concerning a vacation package offered to fans of the Cleveland Browns." "You have got to be kidding me." Bill looked at her and shook his head. She smiled back at him. The light here seemed very strange. She dropped her purse and looked down at it beside her shoe. She looked up — Bill was coming toward her. She felt her hand reaching out but he was too slow, he was remarkably slow, and when she collapsed, she tried to let her knees go down first, because any other way, her body said, there was the problem of her head and the floor.

The world spun back, and everyone was up in arms.

At least five men were above her, fanning her.

"I'm fine," she said several times.

They let her up into a sitting position. She told them she was okay.

"Just a glass of water," she said, "and the room. I'll be fine." Someone had called an ambulance and she told Bill to send it away and he spoke with the EMTs and persuaded them to go. They turned and trudged out of the lobby, looking disappointed, carrying their big cases and their defibrillators.

When Bill finally got them into the room, she went straight to bed and closed her eyes. She heard Bill say from the bathroom, "That was interesting," before she fell asleep.

When she woke up, it was dark.

Bill was in the bed beside her, watching television, volume low.

He glanced down and saw that her eyes were open.

"Well, hello," he said. "Elvis has returned to the building."

She sat up in bed, her back against the headboard, and ran both hands across her face and through her hair.

"You have some kind of royal speed hangover?"

"I'm hungry," she said. "I think. I feel like the last day of my life was a movie."

"We have some food in the other room."

"How long have I been sleeping?" she asked.

"Pretty long," he said. "But tomorrow we'll be fine. You've just redefined the whole genre of nightmare travel stories."

"It was like I was...I don't know. I felt like I was watching myself through a glass case."

She ran her hands through her hair again, then turned and looked at her husband. His bare chest and face were both lit by the TV. He had his glasses on. She imagined him here in the room with her for all the hours she had been asleep. She thought of him at the phone, ordering food, trying to think of what she would like to have. Glass case or no glass case, she had written all those things. Her mind was pushing her, over and over again, to relive everything. She wanted it to end. She needed it to end.

"Bill," she said.

"Renee," he said.

"I'm so sorry," she said. "I'm so sorry for everything."

"Collapsing doesn't count as your fault."

She was silent.

"What?" he said. "That was a bad day, Renee. That's fine. Forget it. Think of it as the extra cost of chasing the sun."

"No."

"What, then?"

"I'm so sorry."

Bill smiled, shook his head. "Stop apologizing and tell me what you're apologizing for, Renee," he said. He sat up and muted the television. He turned to her and put his hand on her shoulder. "Come on. Out with it."

PATRICK SOMERVILLE

"I'm sorry," she said, and she put her hand over her mouth. "Oh my God," she said. The smallest of steps toward it, and this was happening.

He must have been able to see the whites of her eyes and the way she was looking at him sideways. She was crying. His eyes changed.

"Oh God," she said, shaking her head. "I can't even say it. The words don't even sound —"

"What, Renee?" he said, louder.

She looked at him intently, hoping he would simply understand. Or that by some twist of fate had always known. Or had read her notebook while she slept.

He didn't know. She could see by his waiting eyes that he didn't know. "When I say them in my mind, it's like they can't be real," she said, wiping at her nose. "The words, I mean. I have — there have been so many times when I've wanted to…"

"You have to tell me, honey," he said. "I'm listening. Tell me. What is it?"

She closed her eyes.

"I have another son."

6

Once, Matt went to jail. It was a bar fight. Up until about five seconds before it started, he didn't have a clue he was about to be involved. He was sitting at the bar with a woman whom he'd met that night. Things were not going well. She'd told him that she was a hairdresser and had added nothing else, and that basically ended the entire line of conversation. You were pretty much fucked in conversation if "hairdresser" was where you stopped. They'd already talked about his job. What was left?

Still, she looked like she wanted him to solve the riddle of the conversation and figure out a way to keep it going, and he was trying to come up with something that would open a door. Typically he was not strong with such things. He liked her — he liked the way she drank, the bottle a little to the side, and he liked her laugh, which was brighter and louder than what he would have expected, based on the few dry comments she'd made since they started talking. She was not a down-on-her-luck person. There was something a little bit brighter about her than anyone else in the place. She's maybe five years older than me, he thought. Then, out of the corner of his eye, he saw a form appear, and he turned and looked up at the man standing before him. "That's a pretty girl you're talking to," he said, and then he punched Matt in the side of the head and knocked him off the bar stool.

It didn't take Matt long to stand up. The man was bigger — six three or six four, with shoulders like a horse's — but he was old. Matt knew that there was a special strategy to fighting older men. They could be like armored tanks and invulnerable, strong in unnatural, limitless ways, able to endure any punishment. But then you found the right place to hit them, and they were done. He looked about fifty-five. He had a silver mustache and his forearms were all tatted up. Everyone in the bar was silent, watching to see what Matt would do. Matt picked his hat up, then touched his head and felt the blood in his hair. He said, "She is pretty," and the two of them went outside and about fifteen people followed. The big man walked in front of him, and as they moved, Matt looked down at his opponent's black sport sandals.

None of Matt's friends were there, out in the parking lot. He looked over at his truck, thought of simply walking to it and driving off. The man said, "I haven't liked you for the last twenty-five minutes or so."

"You don't have much reason for that."

"I don't like the way you sit," said the man. Matt saw that he made a fist with his right hand and let the left hang limp. "I also don't like the way you gesture."

"Okay," Matt said. "Work out your feelings."

The man stepped forward, right arm cocked. It was all so slow Matt wondered whether the man was trying to trick him, but he wasn't, and Matt easily stepped away from the punch, to the side, and as the man went by, he stomped his right boot down with everything he had on the man's ankle and heard the whole thing crackle. The man collapsed to the concrete, hollering, and Matt kicked him hard in the kidney, twice, punched him in the side of the head, right where he'd punched Matt, then walked to his truck, got in, turned on his lights, reversed out of his spot, and drove away.

He got pulled over five minutes later.

"You broke quite a few of that man's personal bone belongings," the cop said to him through the window, and then he took him in.

That was the only time he'd ever been behind bars, unless you counted the foster homes, and he didn't, because there weren't bars. All throughout the fight, he'd felt nothing. The whole night in the can, he'd felt nothing. In the morning, after bail, walking away from the building and driving home, he'd felt nothing. In his bathroom he looked a little closer at his head and found that the cut was small, although the lump was large. He took a shower, washed his hair gingerly, then watched the second quarter of the Packers game and scrubbed his toilet during halftime.

He crossed the Mississippi around noon, in La Crosse, and smiled to himself, thinking of Glen's comment about the tornado that had come through.

An unexpected relevance now. The Mississippi was its dark, wide, massive self, barge-laden, and he didn't pay it much attention as he crossed the bridge. He'd seen it before. It was a river, only big.

Minnesota looked and felt much the same as Wisconsin. He drove for an hour with the radio off, then stopped at an old roadside place and had a hamburger and french fries. He asked the old cook about the town of Walton, and the cook told him that he knew it well. It was only another forty-five minutes or so more, straight west.

Matt thought of asking the cook about this Darren Roberts, too, but he decided not to. It wouldn't be hard to find the house, and Matt didn't like the idea of spreading his own story all across the countryside. Instead he ate the rest of his meal in silence, paid in cash and left it at his table, and was driving again in twenty minutes. He tried to tune the radio to something he liked but could find few stations, and he looked out across the flatland of southern Minnesota and thought about his house at that very moment and tried to imagine it; he wondered whether Marissa had called in sick again or if she'd gone to work. Maybe it was empty. He thought then about his own work. Right now Ken had his shift. Right now he was supposedly in Tennessee, weeping over somebody's grave.

The rest of the way, he thought about nothing.

It turned out it was a tiny forgotten town, not just a small town, and it was much dirtier than Sturgeon Bay. You could see the whole thing from the right angle. Walton, Minnesota. On the way in, Matt drove past a dead factory of some sort. It had thousands of rectangular windows, every one of them either broken or coated in dust and grime. Beside the structure an enormous mechanical creature had died, arms and legs raised up to the sky. Everything was rusted out. There were heaps of scrap metal on either side of the old factory and a vast, empty parking lot. Behind it, to the north, the land was flat and spread out forever. Matt was glad he didn't live here.

He passed a grocery store and a gas station, then found himself in the middle of town, riding along Main Street. There were some dusty bars here and there, a few restaurants, and a few shops. An old man was sitting in a chair on the sidewalk, staring at the road. So far he was the only human being Matt had seen since entering the city limits. He thought about pulling over and asking the old man where to find the road he was looking for, but decided not to. If you drove long enough in a town like this, you'd always sail right by what you were looking for. So he did it. He cruised to the very end of the Walton town line, turned the truck around in someone's driveway, turned down a street that took him south, drove all the way he could in that direction, turned the truck back around, and went past Main Street again, this time north. It was only a few blocks up that he encountered Ferris Street. He turned right, and about seven seconds later he was parked at the address Mary Landower had given him.

The house was small like Hannah's but more decrepit. Just like the difference between the towns themselves. One quaint, one not at all. The siding was old and dirty; it looked like it was once a cool yellow, but now it was just dirt brown. There was a rickety set of wooden stairs leading up to the front door and no car parked in the driveway. Friday afternoon probably meant that this Darren was at work, if he worked. Matt looked at the clock: 2:30.

He climbed the rickety stairs and knocked, but there was no answer.

He went back to the truck, pulled his hat down, crossed his arms, cracked his window, and closed his eyes. He thought to himself: either be here or not, just make it one or the other.

The big man pressed charges, but different charges. At first they said it was going to be a felony because so many bones had been broken, but when the man found this out, he went to the courthouse himself, plastered up in his big white cast and using a cane, then to the police station, and told everyone he could find that he did not want any felony charges coming against Matt. "If we're talking about a fight between two human beings with nothing at all but the two human beings involved, that's what's called a misdemeanor. I don't care if he did a levitating jujitsu maneuver on me. It's a misdemeanor." Matt heard about this conversation from a friend at the police station a few days after he made bail. He never saw the man again and never heard a word from him. All he ended up getting was community service from a misdemeanor assault.

That was at a different time, a few years before Marissa, back when television was still satisfying and back when the love he had for Marissa had been only a latent want not linked to Marissa at all — more of a hole that made him furtive and forced him out to such bars and into such situations. He lived in a tiny apartment above a Laundromat in downtown St. Helens. He worked all the time. It wasn't very far from the time he'd tried to find his parents, actually, and the time he'd run headlong into that answering machine.

"You don't look like the UPS man, son."

The voice was woven in and out of a dream, but even in the dream Matt knew it was real and that he was dreaming. He opened his eyes.

"I said, you don't look like the UPS man."

Standing outside his window was a scrawny fortysomething man with a goatee. He was wearing a T-shirt and a pair of jeans, and he had his sunglasses on the brim of his hat. Matt straightened up. Looking down, he saw that the man was holding a case of beer in his right hand. He looked neither friendly nor particularly hostile. Just interested in Matt's answer. Interested in Matt.

"I'm not," Matt said.

"You waitin' for me?"

"Are you Darren Roberts?"

"Who wants to know?"

"I do," Matt said. "I am waiting for you."

"Okay," he said. He looked past Matt, at the *Gazetteer* — this one the whole United States — open on the seat. "Great. What do you want and what's your damn name?"

Matt rubbed his hand over his face, then nodded at the door. Darren took a few steps back and Matt got out. He held out his hand to shake, and Darren looked down at it for a moment, then took it with his free hand. "My name's Matt Bishop," Matt said. "This is gonna be a long story."

"Tell me the short version."

Matt looked up at Darren's house, then back at Darren. "Okay," he said. "I'm looking for something you might have. I'm married to the daughter of a woman named Caroline Francis."

The man smiled quickly at the mention of Caroline's name, then leaned backward, away from Matt, and made a little O with his lips and whistled out of them. "Whoa, cowboy. This is gonna be a long story, ain't it?"

"It can be," Matt said.

The man waited.

"You got a cradle in there? A cradle that used to be Caroline's?"

"I know what cradle you're talkin' about."

A quick jet of relief washed through Matt.

"That's what I'm looking for. No questions asked." The questions Matt was telling him that he didn't have to ask were the questions Matt had been asking himself since he started driving west.

Did Caroline already know Darren before she left the family?

Did she leave *for* him?

That didn't seem to fit into the notion Matt had of her as a free spirit, running away from people and duties and responsibilities. But then again maybe the easiest way of fleeing your own life is to daisy-chain your way out through a series of smaller and smaller commitments. That way at least you have some excuses. For yourself or others. The reverse-stepladder method of fucking people.

This thinking had led Matt up to one other question as well: if indeed Caroline had known this man, and if indeed she had left the family for him, was he the same man who'd broken into the house that night, ten days later?

Matt was curious and wanted to know. That's why he said, "No questions asked."

"What'd you say your name was?" Darren said.

"Matt Bishop."

"And what's your lady's name?"

"Marissa."

"Marissa," Darren Roberts repeated, looking past Matt. "I'd forgotten that name. But that was it."

"You were married to Caroline, then?" Matt said.

"Yes," said the man. "I was. Caroline. One crazy bitch. Now *that* woman was an actual cowboy."

"And the cradle?"

"How far you come?"

"From Wisconsin."

"All right," he said. "Come inside." He held up the beer and didn't smile one bit. "Lucky for us, I just picked up another case of Dom Pérignon."

7

Inside, the living room was a small box, but tidier than Matt had expected, considering. There was a white couch and a clean coffee table. The rug looked like it had been vacuumed recently. On another table there was a blue lamp with at least a 100-watt bulb burning inside, and overhead, the ceiling lights were equally bright. Things smelled of deodorizer, and beneath the smell Matt thought he could detect old cigarette smoke, too. It felt like a doctor's office from 1979.

Darren motioned to the couch and disappeared around a corner with his beer. Matt heard the sounds of doors opening and closing, and after a moment there was a bark and a mangy mutt came tearing around the corner, wagging its tail and skipping around Matt. It licked his hands and tried to jump on him in excitement, and Matt stroked the steely hair on its head. It had a little beard, wet with saliva and crud. When it turned to go back to Darren, Matt saw that it wasn't neutered, and he looked for a moment at the stretched skin around its huge balls.

"He's nice, don't worry," said Darren, coming back around the corner.

"I bet."

He had two cold beers in one hand, against his chest; in the other he held a small black case. He went to the La-Z-Boy next to the couch. He opened a drawer in the coffee table and pulled out two coasters. Then he cracked both beers and slid one over to Matt, on the coaster. The dog, still wagging its tail, began frantically moving between the two men, unsure who was going to give him more attention.

"What's his name?"

"Darren."

"Your dog's got the same name as you?"

"Long story," said Darren. "And there is no short version."

Matt picked up the beer and took a sip.

"So now I'm wondering," said Darren, leaning back into the seat with his own beer, looking up at the ceiling, "how in the hell you found me. If you don't mind me asking."

"I had a conversation with Mary Landower," said Matt. "Caroline's sister."

Darren nodded now, then let his eyes rest on Matt. He was still wearing his baseball cap, and his sunglasses were still resting on the brim. "I figured it must have been her. You sure as shit didn't talk to Caroline."

"No."

"Mary tell you where she is?" Darren asked.

"She said Indonesia."

"That makes sense," said Darren. His hand went to his goatee and he scratched it. "That makes sense."

"This cradle —"

"Hold on," said Darren.

He reached down for the black case and picked it up, into his lap. He cracked it open. Matt saw him messing around inside it, but he couldn't see what was in it. Then Darren brought out a gun and rested it in his lap.

He put the case down beside his chair.

Matt watched him tensely for a few moments as Darren positioned the gun in his lap, then picked up his beer.

When he looked at Matt, he was casual and seemed surprised by Matt's look. He said, "I just thought you might be here to kill me." Darren moved his lips around like he was eating something sour, then said, "Are you?"

Matt said, "Not at all."

"For the break-in," he said, "and all that. Or any other revenge scenarios your wife may have been dreaming up for years. I understand human fantasy. Well."

"I'm here to find that cradle," Matt said.

"Okay, fine," said Darren. "And you know what? You did. The thing's in the basement." He waved the gun over his shoulder, then set it back in his lap. "You win the big prize."

Darren the Dog stared at Matt along with Darren the Human.

Matt leaned back and tried to relax. "That's all I want," he said.

"But why would you want it so badly? I'm curious."

"My wife," he said. "She wants it. We're having a baby. She remembers it."

"So she sent you out to hell knows where to find it."

"That's right."

"And that's all?"

"That's all."

"Nothing more."

"Nothing more."

Darren laughed then. It was high-pitched and weaselly. "Pregnant women," he said. "Am I right?"

Matt said nothing.

"Do me a favor and say one more time that you're only here to get that thing."

"I just want the cradle," Matt said. "I don't care about anything else."

"You see, I can perceive lies of all kinds," said Darren. "One of my gifts is to know whenever someone's lying to me. I see right through anyone. I'm amazing, in a way."

"You can see then that I'm not lying."

Darren sighed. His hand went down to his dog's head and he scratched it. Then the hand went over to the case, and he put the gun back inside, clicked it closed, and set it down beside the dog.

"Look," he said. "We had a little break-in here a while back. My apologies. It looks like a small town but it's complex as shit. And in all honesty, when any history having to do with Caroline comes knocking on your door, it's not exactly a dumb idea to arm yourself, if you know what I mean. But I believe you. You are a rather sincere-looking individual, you know that? I doubt I would have even needed my amazing powers of perception."

It had happened so fast that he didn't have much time to react beyond some rudimentary scared-shitlessness.

"Can we see it?" Matt said. "I'll take it and get out of your hair, then leave you alone."

Darren raised his beer up and drained the entire second half into his gullet. He set the empty can down on the coaster and said, "Of course there is the small matter of price."

Matt kept watching him.

"But let's go have a looky, shall we?"

Darren led him through the kitchen and then down a thin flight of stairs. He pulled a string at the bottom and a lightbulb came on; Matt saw shadows and a small concrete room, musty, with piles of boxes and furniture against all the walls. Darren moved aside part of a table and went farther in, then pulled another lightbulb on. Darren the Dog trotted down the stairs, wagging his tail. "Now let me see here," said Darren, hands on hips. "Aha."

He stepped into a corner and started pulling on a mound.

Matt took a step forward, but there wasn't enough room. He could only watch as Darren threw aside a pile of old clothes, moved a box, and cleared a path. Then he dragged the mound out into the center of the small room.

He peeled off an old mattress cover from the top of the mound and threw it aside, and there was the cradle.

The stain was dark but so old now it had no gloss. There was an old tape player inside, and Darren leaned down and took it out, then stepped back to let Matt see the whole thing. It was solid and sturdy-looking, low to the ground on two sleigh feet. Matt knelt before it. He put his hand on the top of the cradle and rocked it once. About thirty thin tube slats made up the two sides, and on the headboard there was an elaborate engraving, stained darker, almost black. It was a floral design, with leaves and thin vines wrapping like the arms of an octopus. There was no mattress in the bottom — only a wicker weave. Matt ran his hand along one smooth sideboard and then stood up.

"Okay," he said.

"Indeed, there it is," said Darren. "And I will sell it to you for the low, low price of one thousand dollars cash."

Matt looked at him with sleepy eyes. He looked down at the cradle, then back at Darren. "It's not worth a tenth of that."

"Worth?" said Darren. "What is *worth?*"

Matt looked back down at the cradle. "Five hundred," he said.

"Ah," said Darren. "A bargaining man. Okay. Yes. I change my price to nine hundred seventy."

"Six hundred."

"Let's say we meet in the middle," said Darren, "at seven fifty."

Matt squatted down beside the cradle once more. He imagined his son inside it. He reached a hand out and started rocking it, and now the dog came up and sat beside him, its tail wagging across the dirty concrete floor. The pleasure. That was what the cost was. That was the definition of *worth. Matter* was somewhere in there, too. Worth and matter. Darren had meant something more cynical about the marketplace. What he didn't understand was that five hundred dollars was nothing when it came to the invisible mass of life. Seven hundred dollars was nothing. Eight hundred was nothing. These were memories of being a living thing. Being able to drive home with it, give it to Marissa, and then for everything to suddenly be over, and for him to be able to sleep, was much better than anything this small man could imagine. Then time would start going forward again.

Matt stood up.

"This town have a bank?" he asked.

Matt withdrew the cash from an ATM back on Main Street, then walked back down toward Ferris Street. On the way there, he'd stopped thinking about what good might come from the cradle's return and had begun to think about Darren again, and something he'd said back at the house.

Pregnant women. Am I right?

So now it seemed obvious. The marketplace.

Caroline hadn't made Darren steal the cradle because it had any particular cash value or sentimental value to her — she'd sent him into the house to take it because of its utilitarian value. She'd sent him in to take it because she had been pregnant or planned to be pregnant again.

With Darren. She'd left Marissa and Glen because she was going to start again somewhere else. Her version of escape was to begin.

It was simple, but it left damage behind that she had to keep moving away from. What kind of woman, Matt wondered, would do this? What kind of person? It was the opposite of Marissa, whose world had become one singular laser beam of attention. If he were to suggest it to her, she would not be able to mentally process the concept. Begin but never stay? Also, if this story was true, where was the child?

If there was a child.

It wasn't dusk yet, but dusk was coming. Matt saw a pay phone. Leaning against a light pole, he deposited the quarters and dialed home. Marissa answered after one ring.

"Hi, baby," she said. "Is this a you-got-it call?"

"No," Matt said. "Not yet. But I might soon."

"Really?" He could hear her eyes go wide.

"Maybe. I'm not sure yet." He cleared his throat, looked down at the ground. He was not used to lying to his wife. "I've gotta go a few more places. The truck's getting some miles."

"Should I ask you where you are right now?"

"Probably not," Matt said, looking at the house.

"Okay," she said. "Dad and I are going to see a movie later on. That's all."

"Did you go to work today?"

"No. I just hurt all over. Every place I go is uncomfortable. I was lying on top of a bed of pillows on the couch and I couldn't even stay there."

Matt imagined her there, splayed out like a queen, with every pillow in the house beneath her.

"So you're not going to be back tonight."

"I might be," he said. "I still don't know."

"Okay," she said. "I'm glad that it's working."

"All right," he said. "I love you. I'll talk to you soon."

"Okay. Be careful."

He hung up the phone and walked back to Darren's house.

He knocked at the front door and heard the dog barking. No one came, though. After a few more knocks, he went around the house and found it had a small backyard. Darren was sitting on a patio chair with another beer. When Matt came around the corner, Darren looked up and said, "I thought you may have reneged."

"No," said Matt. "Here." He handed him the fat pile of money. For a moment the number of hours of work it constituted surfaced in his mind like a submarine and startled him. He beat back the feeling.

Darren took the money, looked at it, looked at Matt, and stuffed it all into his back pocket.

"I'll help you carry it up."

The two men carried the cradle up the stairs carefully — Matt went backward. The dog was moving around behind him, and he had to stop a couple of times and kick backward lightly to get him to move. Darren yelled at Darren a few times and told him he was a sonofabitch. Out on the street, they could just get the cradle inside the truck's door. Matt angled it and had it sitting in the seat. He reached over and pulled the seat belt across it, and Darren laughed and shook his head when he saw that happening.

"How about another beer before you go, then?" he asked, hands on his hips. "Now that we're close friends and all."

"Okay," Matt said. "I could do that."

They went back around the house.

Evening was coming finally, and it was cooling off. Matt was tired and took the beer gladly from the man who not an hour ago vaguely threatened him with a gun. He just couldn't tell about Darren. He was clean when he was supposed to be a slob and smarter than he was supposed to be, too. And yet in him Matt sensed something deeply selfish. It was something in the way he joked, something in the way his eyes went up when he thought, or how he shook his head or scratched at his little beard or wore his sunglasses on his head. Something in the way he'd received him. Matt didn't know. Had the man been hurt by Caroline in the same way Glen had been? He didn't seem like the kind of person you could hurt. He just seemed like the kind of person who hurt other people. You could get hurt only if your heart ever pointed outward.

Matt said, "So what do you do?"

"Not a lot," he said. "I went to an interview today about fifty miles from here. I've been painting houses in town, but there's better work in Rochester. What do you do?"

"Factory work. Chemical plant."

"Steady?"

"I've been there eight years."

"Sounds just delightful," said Darren. Then he burped loudly, and the noise brought Darren the Dog to the back door to check things out through the screen, ears up.

"How often do voices in your head talk to you?" Darren asked.

"Never."

"Not even your own voice?"

"I do think, if that's what you mean."

"But how can that voice be you, if you're the one who's listening? Do you see my point here, Matt?"

"I've never thought about it."

Darren scrunched up his lips, nodded, took a long pull from his beer. "People speak to me," he said. "They do. I thought for some time it was only one using different voices, as in ventriloquism, et cetera. But now I'm not so sure."

Matt looked at the fence and worked on his beer.

"Want another one?"

"Okay."

Darren got up, went inside, and came back with more beers.

"Interesting story," Darren said, "along those same lines. I once tried to become a shaman. There are whole courses for it, you know."

"What does one do to be a shaman?"

"Had to go all the way to India," said Darren. "Yes," he said, nodding. "You don't see it if you look at me. I bet you're wondering what I'm talking about. Voices, shamanism. Let me tell you. Everything with being a shaman didn't exactly fucking work out, granted, but beyond that I like to think of myself as a self-educated philosopher."

"What kind of —"

"Now I went all the way and I'm a nihilist," Darren said, "which basically makes me the be-all of philosophers. I believe in nothing. After a long and arduous path of studying, I've come upon that. What I realized was that actually I've always been that, and it just took me reading about seven hundred books at about one word per hour to finally figure out what it was called."

"Okay," Matt said. "Wonderful."

"You see, it's about the human condition," Darren said. "I never judge anyone. That makes me special; most people do. My mother, for example. That woman just hates everyone. She's stuck in that, she'll never get out of that. I don't think shit about anything. All I ever do is watch people operate."

"You mind if I ask you a question?" Matt said.

"No, I am not a multimillionaire."

"What happened?" Matt said, ignoring him. "Back then? With Caroline?"

Darren raised one corner of his upper lip, then closed one eye.

"Oh yes," he said. "Caroline. Isn't it obvious to you? I don't know. Maybe I don't know what *obvious* is. Definitions are suspicious things. It's not obvious?"

"Some," Matt said. "You met her down in Milwaukee and you left together. Somehow. And then she put you up to robbing Glen's house for her."

"Glen." Darren nodded. "That was his name, wasn't it? Quiet little pushover mouse-person?"

"He's a good man and also my father-in-law."

"Good. What's *good*?"

"Good is good."

"Yeah, well, I guess that fits," said Darren, "as Caroline is not a good woman and I am not a particularly good man. According to the way you're meaning it, at least."

"She left you?"

"She left me. But not for about five years. Then she just took off one night and left me with the kid."

Matt breathed in slowly, then exhaled through his nose, looking down at his boots.

"There's a kid."

"There's a kid," said Darren, "rocked in that very cradle. You're shitting me. You're telling me you didn't know that? What am I, like, the only person who can tell what's going on?"

"How old is he?"

"I think he should be five now."

"Should be?"

"I do some proactive blocking out of some of these things, you've gotta understand."

"Where is he?"

"He's at my mother's now."

"And where is that?"

Darren turned and looked at him.

"You're talking about a person who is basically my wife's brother," said Matt, "if you're wondering why I care."

Darren nodded, breathed in and out once, thinking. "Well, okay. Fine. But it might be the kind of thing better left undisturbed," Darren said. "Just to give you some advice on that. I know you're going to be a father soon. Why don't you worry about that? I usually advocate thinking of history as cement. You know. It gets hard. That's it. That's what I suggest to my clients."

"Why did you give him up?"

"Because I had a life of my own," he said. "Because I don't want no kid wandering around my house. I already have Darren.

But beyond that, from an abstract point of view, if you will. This one Caroline had, he gave me the willies. Never talked. And once Caroline was gone, do you think I had the faintest idea what to do with him? No. Absolutely not. I just told you I didn't care. We sat here together and watched TV. I'm no father. It doesn't fit."

"But you are his father."

"Maybe. That's in doubt. She had a few flings. I'm not convinced one way or the other."

"You were here, he was here. He thinks you're his father."

"He doesn't remember me."

"You couldn't have —"

"Here is the essential truth of this, Matt," Darren said loudly, much more agitated than he'd been. "It doesn't matter. Not in the long run. Let me make manifest my point of view for you. If we were to sit down and tally up every single person in this town, then state, let alone this country, let alone the world, it wouldn't make a difference what happens to him. If you hold anything up alongside that, you come down with exactly zero. And so I said to myself, Hell, if it doesn't matter one way or another, in the same way nothing does, not really, then if I want to live this way, then I'm gonna live this way. Ain't no goddamned little kid going to alter the path that I'm on. I am a motherfucking thinker and I am on a motherfucking path. And I don't give a shit if my path is all alone and terrible, at the very least it's my terrible, and I'm going to walk along on my terrible path all by myself and piss when I want, et cetera. That's how it was done to me and that's how I'm doing it."

About a minute passed after Darren stopped talking.

"You must go to see him, then," Matt said. "At your mother's."

"My mother and I do not talk nor correspond."

"When was the last time you saw him?"

"When I dropped him off."

"When was that?"

"Year and a half ago."

Matt paused. "Mind if I use your bathroom?"

"Go ahead."

Matt got up and opened the screen door. Darren the Dog jumped all over him as he went to the bathroom. Inside, he peed, then looked at himself in the mirror. He was feeling something he didn't recognize.

It felt, in a way, like the good feeling, about the days rolling by — the gratitude.

Except it was turned on its head and reversed in some way, and felt powerful, and dark.

Back in the kitchen, Matt held open the door and said to Darren, "How about another one?"

It took a solid three hours to get him falldown drunk. Twice Matt went into the house to vomit. His other trick to keep up with Darren was to just open a new beer whenever Darren opened a new beer and set his half-full beer down in the grass, as though he had finished it. Darren's final musings on the night came in the form of a huge piss beside his grill and a comment about too many Hispanics moving into town. After that he sat back down in his chair, tilted to the side, and collapsed onto the ground.

Matt considered helping him up and dragging him into bed, but he was drunk, despite his best efforts not to be, and besides, since he'd learned about the kid, he'd been having more and more trouble holding back the urge to stand up and kick Darren in the jaw and watch as every one of his teeth fell out of his face. So it was fine that he would spend the night on the slab of concrete that constituted his porch. Matt let himself into the house and looked around for a desk or a file drawer. In the dining room he stumbled about and found a shoe box full of receipts, but that didn't help him. He went upstairs to the bedroom. It was also neat — the bed was even made. Some bachelor. Matt looked through some drawers and again found nothing. He went back downstairs, to the kitchen. Beneath the silverware he found a drawer that had papers and postcards in it, along with a roll of outdated thirty-two-cent stamps. He shuffled through the cards; at the bottom, he found a birthday card, still tucked inside its envelope. He pulled it out.

On the front there was a pig. Inside, the bold writing said OINK. Beneath it, in a scrawl, the message said, "Happy birthday, Darren. This will be a strong year for Pisces. Your mom."

He slid the card back inside the envelope and looked at the return address. Rensselaer, Indiana. The postmark made it three years old.

Matt copied the address down onto a blank envelope he found, then put the card back at the bottom of the pile, then put the pile back right where he'd found it. Outside he looked disdainfully at Darren again, then went to the half-full beers he'd had around his feet and emptied them out, one by one, into the grass. He put the cans back beneath the chair. Finally, he turned out the light and left Darren in darkness, just a tangled curl of arms and legs. He walked around the outside of the house, got in his truck, and drove away.

He took special care to drive well on his way out of town. He was not sober, not by a long shot. Once he'd gotten a few miles east, he pulled over at a gas station and bought a thirty-two-ounce coffee and a bottle of No-Doz, ate three of the pills in the parking lot, filled up with gas, drove off, and turned the radio up loud and zoned out, spending most of his mental energy on aiming high and not weaving. The cradle was right there beside him, stable with the belt around it; once in a while he found himself touching it. It was past midnight, but if he drove all night he'd be there before the sun came up, or at the very least just as it was coming up.

And he was. Right at sunrise, he was parked three blocks from his house with the engine off.

It can be completely done right now, he said to himself. I can tear this envelope up, even, and walk inside with this in my arms and be the hero. And then time will start.

He had, though, parked this far away from the house, and he knew the reason. The reason was the feeling. It was a fog, lighter than it had been back with Darren but still there, absolutely still there, and it was not at all a joyful celebration of life. It was the same rage.

He thought back to the answering machine, when he'd given up on it before he'd encountered this, and he thought of Darren's bullshit pontifications on the world and on life. That had been it. That man had been the conflagration of all wrong ideas in the universe.

He looked at the cradle. Just walk inside with it in your arms, all will be well.

He was so tired — if he walked inside, he could lay his head down on the pillow beside Marissa, sleep in, eat a big breakfast in the morning, then try to get a Sunday shift to start making up for what he'd spent on the cradle.

He reached into his pocket and looked at the envelope, crumpled now. The address in his wobbly drunken handwriting.

He looked at the cradle.

He started the car, drove past his own home, and got back on the highway, this time heading south.

8

He called Marissa from the motel just past noon and said, "Another day, I think. I'm close."

"You sound tired."

"I've driven a lot," he said. "I'm going to get some sleep now, actually. I just got a motel room."

"It's noon."

"My schedule is not quite a nine-to-five schedule at the moment."

She told him about the movie she'd seen with her father, then talked about what it was like to feel the baby kicking when he wasn't around. She'd had a dream that she'd gone into labor early and had gone to the hospital. She'd told the doctors the baby had to wait for Matt's return, and then a nurse had come in and taken her hand and said, "But you are giving birth to your husband."

"Good Lord," Matt said.

"I know. Thank God I didn't have to watch you crown."

"I'll be back before anything happens," he said. "Don't worry about that."

"All right. Come home soon. I'm missing you. And on top of that I've got a surprise."

"What?"

"The purpose of surprises, Matt."

"Okay," he said. "I'll look forward to it. I'll be home soon. Promise."

He took off his shoes, leaned back on the bed, and closed his eyes.

He didn't wake for six hours. When he did, he shot up with a start and could feel immediately that much more time than he'd planned had passed. Outside it was still light, but the angle of the sun wasn't very high. His muscles were sore, his body was still deep down inside itself, and he had a headache. The No-Doz, probably. His mouth was parched. He slid from the bed and started the shower. He came back out into the room. The cradle was sitting in front of the television set, right where he'd put it when he first came in.

He was ten miles past Rensselaer in a Motel 6. He'd assumed there wouldn't be anything in the town itself and had gone on just a little bit more after seeing the sign. Right across the street there was a Denny's, so after his shower he crossed and went inside and ate at least five heart attacks of eggs, bacon, and waffles, then ordered a chocolate milk shake and sucked it down in the parking lot, sitting on the curb.

He did not know what he planned to do. He was here, though, and at the very least he'd go to the house and see the kid and make sure he was real. From there, they'd talk, and he'd tell her. Then it would be difficult — tell her that her mother had another baby, that she had a little half brother living down in Indiana, that Caroline hadn't left because she hated children but because she'd wanted more. Such things could introduce unexpected complexities. Part of Matt, even though he still felt rage toward Darren for his speech about things mattering and not mattering, agreed with the man a little bit. It would be as though he never found this out.

But then again, he was here.

Matt finished his milk shake, threw it in a trash bin, and walked back to the motel. It was evening now; the light was fading. Suppertime was over. He got in his truck and got back on the highway.

The small streets of Rensselaer reminded him a little of Walton, Minnesota — the shops along the central avenue were run-down and there weren't many people about. The houses were much the same as well. The only real difference Matt felt was a difference in light, in the feeling of the colors. Indiana had a special light. Minnesota had been gray — even the grass. Here there was an orange hue to everything as the sun hung low in the sky and traced a burning line across the top of every structure. There were more trees, and those, too, seemed to have a warm glow in the evening haze. He again used his driving-back-and-forth strategy, looking for the right road. Rensselaer was bigger, and it took him longer, but eventually he found the house. On one side of the road there was vast farmland with alfalfa in the field. The house was on the corner and had more grass than the others around it, even though the structure itself wasn't very big. It was made out of brick and had two big bay windows in the front living room and a dilapidated basketball hoop tilting forward in the driveway. Behind the house there were many trees — Matt could see the leaves and branches high up over the roof.

He went to the door and rang the bell.

Nothing.

He rang again, and again there was no answer. He took a few steps back, then walked into the yard and tried to look through the window. The curtains were all drawn. He crossed his arms and looked back at his truck and could see the cradle through the windshield, his passenger waiting patiently. Without really thinking about it, he meandered around the side of the house and walked along the low wooden fence that defined the backyard, letting his hand skim across the ancient twisted 4x4s, looking casually over his shoulder as the rear came into view.

He could see nothing through the back windows — the house looked empty. He stayed where he was anyway, hands on the fence. I could leave, and this would never have happened. . . .

There was the boy.

It was a little white circle in the upstairs window. The face was looking out at Matt just as the cat had in Sturgeon Bay, unmoving, ghostlike. Matt could see his arms hanging straight down at his side.

Then the boy's hand came up. He was waving.

After a moment of watching this, he looked over his shoulder at the rest of Rensselaer, looked again at the window and the waving boy.

Matt waved back.

Marissa, usually rock steady, changed on the day of the wedding. She was a rock before and she was a rock after, but she became a different rock, shaped with different edges. She never cried before.

Not once. But that day in Glen's backyard, with her all in white, fifteen people sitting in collapsible chairs watching them, Marissa's grandma and grandpa sitting in the front row, she'd wept. The whole damned day. The morning, the hours before, all through the ceremony, then at the reception, and even on the dance floor. For the entire day she was occupied by some degree of crying. It was at its peak as they stood before the minister beneath the floral trellis. She held both his hands and looked into his eyes, hers red and puffed up, with tears pouring from them. She had a Kleenex stuffed into the top of her dress. Through the morning Matt had smiled along with it and had not thought too much about it, but there beneath the trellis, he'd begun, for the first time, to get worried. He knew what tears of happiness looked like; he knew how smiles broke through them here and there. And maybe some of Marissa's tears were tears of happiness that day. But certainly not all of them. He saw so much pain that day. And holding her hands there, as the minister spoke, he realized that love was making him into far more than he ever could have been on his own. He could have sailed around the earth in a hot-air balloon or been a scientist inside a laboratory solving cancer and still those things would have been nothing compared to what she needed him to be, compared to the vessel she was turning him into. It was as though she had held all her pain and her anger deep inside herself until the day she was certain she'd never be alone again. Once that was confirmed, she'd been able to let go.

Had it all been beautiful, Matt would have wept, too. The truth was that it scared him. Her in her white dress, unable to talk, had been frightening. Later he'd had too much to drink and had just barely avoided doing the chicken dance. That he'd even considered it was as sure a sign as any that he had not been himself.

She finally stopped crying late that night, when they were both in bed. Out of the dress and in her pajamas, Marissa smiled at him. They'd already made love, and Matt, exhausted, was looking through his tuxedo, trying to find his wallet.

"It's two in the morning," she said. "What do you need your wallet for?"

"I think I lost it."

"Why did you have your wallet in your pocket for your wedding, Matt?"

"I have no answer to that question," he said, throwing the pants down onto the floor.

"Come here."

Matt looked at her. She had her arms out. He went to the bed and lay down beside her, and she put her arms around him.

"What was all the crying, baby?" he asked. "You scared me up there. It didn't look like you were feeling joy."

"I don't know what I was feeling. I feel joy now, though."

It was nine o'clock when the boat of a car pulled into the driveway, and the light was almost totally gone. Matt was waiting back inside the truck, beside the cradle. He left it immediately and approached the driveway before the woman had a chance to get to her front door. There, from a few feet behind her, he said, "Excuse me, ma'am," and she turned and put her hand up to her throat, startled.

"Good Jesus," she said after a moment. She shook her head, not entirely relaxed, and adjusted her big, bubbly glasses.

In the low light Matt couldn't quite see the color of her hair, but it was big, whatever it was. She had a massive purse, too, hanging down underneath her armpit. She kept her hand up by her throat. "Can I help you?" she said. Her voice was deep.

PATRICK SOMERVILLE

"I'm sorry to bother you, ma'am," Matt said. "I've just been to see your son. My name is Matt Bishop. I'm married to Marissa, the sister of that little boy in your house."

Now a long, quiet stare. The hand slowly fell from the throat and went back, awkwardly, to the woman's side. It then passed over her belt and went to the purse, and she started digging around. The hand came out with what looked like a box of cigarettes. The woman took a step forward without pulling one out. She said, "And."

"That's all," Matt said. "Up until last night I didn't know he existed."

"And Darren sent you here?"

"No. I came without him saying."

"How did you know where to find me?"

Matt looked back over his shoulder, at the truck. He sighed, turned back. "I found your address on a birthday card after he passed out."

The woman laughed once, like a bark, then chuckled lowly.

Matt watched her shoulders move up and down as she did. Then the cigarette came out of the pack and went up to her mouth, and she lit it.

"So you want him."

"Excuse me?"

"If you want him," she said, "you can have him. I don't want him anymore."

"Who?" Matt said.

"Who do you think I mean? Darren?"

Matt wished he could see the woman's face better. Now it was only a dark spot, whereas the boy's had been lit preternaturally in the window. All he could see well was the glow of the cigarette's tip.

"I can't take him," Matt said. "That's not —"

"And here I was, thinking you were a dark angel come to rescue me from my son's idiocy."

"I thought at the very least," Matt said, "my wife, Marissa, should know that he exists. That's what this is about."

"Okay, then," the woman said. She swung her head and her big hair and looked at her front door, then turned back. "Let's go make sure he exists, even though you saw him through the window."

There was something in her movement and her voice, in that last sentence, that made Matt realize just how drunk she was. The way she'd been able to cover it up through the beginning of the conversation made him think, too, that this was not amateur drinking. This was a lifetime's work.

He followed her. At the door she messed around with her keys for quite some time, and he was close enough to smell the strong perfume coming off of her. With hair, she was taller than he. Without hair, she wasn't.

Inside, the air-conditioning was on high, so strong it was chilly. She flipped on the light and continued walking, and Matt stood. The living room was neat and tidy, although it didn't have the same sterility that Darren's did. There were two cats lying together on the sofa, in each other's arms. One, a tabby, looked up at them, and the other didn't move. The woman disappeared through a doorway, and Matt followed her. He found her in the kitchen, leaning down and looking into the refrigerator. When he came around the corner, she twisted her head and said, "I'm Susan, by the way. You want something? Dinner? You'd think I would have eaten something by now."

"I'm fine," Matt said.

She pulled out a cucumber, brought it to the countertop, and started cutting it. She was well over sixty, but Matt could see she'd once been astoundingly beautiful. A part of it remained. She was wearing a long, loose dress and sandals. She'd gotten a new cigarette for herself at some point, and now she leaned over the cucumber and started slicing it. She'd lost the glasses somewhere. "You have a certain look to you, you know," she said. When Matt didn't respond, the woman took in a lungful of air, leaned her head up toward the ceiling, and yelled, "Joseph! Come down here!"

There was a bang like he jumped off of something, and then Matt listened as the footsteps moved across a room above, then came to the stairs, then trundled down the stairs. The woman pointed with the knife. "You see?" she said. "QED. Existence."

Matt turned. The little boy was standing in the doorway, wearing a pair of white briefs and a white T-shirt. He also had on a pair of Strawberry Shortcake socks. His hair was black and messy, and he stood still, looking up at Matt, arms down at his sides.

"He doesn't talk," Susan said.

Matt found himself squatting down. He stayed there, looking at the boy across the room. He thought of holding out a hand to shake, but of course that would be ridiculous. "Hi," he said instead.

The boy turned and left the room.

Matt heard him go back upstairs.

"He doesn't talk," the woman said, "and I for one find it quite eerie."

Matt stood and turned back to her. "Doesn't talk at all?"

"He said hello once," said Susan. "Other than that, no." She was starting to cut again.

"Are you his guardian?" Matt said.

"No."

"Who is?"

"I'd imagine Darren is still," she said. "I haven't checked."

"You haven't checked?"

"No, I haven't checked."

"What about school? You have to know."

"He's not in school."

"How old is he?"

"He's five."

"So is he starting school, then?" Matt asked. "In the fall?"

Now the woman was leaning forward on the countertop, holding a sliced cucumber in front of her mouth like it was a potato chip. "You seem to be understanding the problem."

"I'm not," Matt said.

"Let me add the last piece of the equation," she said. "I am getting married in four weeks. I have a honeymoon to go to in Costa Rica. After that I would not mind taking a trip to California, to visit my sister. From there, I don't know. James and I may move. We like it better in Florida. None of these things fit properly with him."

"Those sound like lovely plans."

"I am not going to do this," she said. "Any of this. I am done. Officially."

"You can't just be done," Matt said.

"I raised my child," she said. "This one's not mine. I am done."

"What, then?" Matt said. "You'll throw him away on garbage day?"

The woman smiled a little and came around the corner of the countertop, a new cucumber slice in her hand. She took a drag from the cigarette, then took a bite, then sat down at the kitchen table. "I knew you were coming," she said. She nodded at another chair.

"How exactly did you know I was coming?"

"My psychic," she said. "I heard about you last week."

"What did you hear?"

"That somebody was going to come and take him away and be his father."

Now she turned and started rooting around in a low cupboard behind the table. Matt didn't move to sit with her. After a moment she turned and had a bottle of whiskey and two glasses. She set them down and filled them both and put the bottle on the table.

"No, thank you," Matt said.

The woman took his cup and poured his whiskey into her own.

"I knew you were coming," said the woman. "You're just in time. Good for you. Congratulations." She sipped.

"You haven't the faintest idea who I am," Matt said, "and now you're trying to give me a child."

"I *do* know who you are," she said to her glass. "You're his brother."

"I'm his brother like I'm your brother."

"No," she said, looking up, shaking her head. "Not quite." She tipped the glass back and drank half the whiskey. She set the glass down with a thunk. "It's a little more than that, isn't it?"

He was back in his room by ten o'clock. He lay on the bed, staring up at the ceiling, television on, sounds of a telephone conversation coming through the wall. It was a man's voice. He wasn't yelling, but it had a persistent strength to it. When the noise got filtered by the wall, it turned into a trumpet with a mute being played sixty feet away — the same note, over and over again.

Come back in the morning. That's what the woman had said. Come back in the morning, and you can take him with you.

She'd almost said it with a smile on her face; like a test, like a tease. All he felt was rage, the same as he'd felt the day before while driving. That anyone could do this, that people could be this. Better for this boy, Joe, to have never been born. It would have saved him the trouble of having to realize so soon people's indifference to their situations. Or to anyone else's.

Because of the feeling, he knew he was a long way away from sleep. He got out of the bed and went across the room to the cradle, which he touched lightly, then rocked. He was standing right in front of the television; some pundit was talking into the camera, holding a pencil, pointing it at someone else. The man said, "She is not and should not be this nation's moral center," and the camera switched and showed another man, and he said, "No one ever asked her to be." Matt looked into the man's eyes and remembered Don Kincaid and his wife, Lucille, the couple who'd taken him when he was nine years old and the couple with whom he'd stayed for nearly two years. They were not particularly bad people and had treated him with a distanced fondness; Lucille had never taken him into her arms and hugged him like he was her son, but she'd touched him on the shoulder when she wanted him to clean up his messes and she'd even sung songs to him from time to time. Don worked at a bank somewhere. They took him to church every Sunday. He hadn't had many friends, but it was the first time in his life he'd felt a sense that the world could be the same thing for a long period of time, that the ground didn't necessarily always have to rumble and shift underneath you. Once, they went to the beach; Matt didn't remember where. Something told him it had been Lake Michigan, but he thought now he might be inserting it after seeing the lake during this trip. More likely it had been somewhere like Lake Geneva. He remembered many tourists, and he remembered Don, wearing goggles, standing on a dock in a pair of blue swimming trunks that matched his own blue swimming trunks, the water trickling down through the silver hair on his chest. He remembered Don telling him to wait where he was because he had a surprise, then disappearing down the dock, then coming back a minute later with another pair of goggles. He said, "Are you ready?" and Matt nodded his head that he was. Don jumped into the water feetfirst. When he came up, he fixed the goggles on his face and said, "Okay, you next," and Matt hadn't hesitated to jump in just beside him, laughing because he knew Don had expected him to wait a long time and have to think it over and be tentative, because that's how he usually was. It had been his little trick. When he came up, Don was laughing, too, and he helped Matt put the goggles on right, and together they swam around and looked at the rocks and mud and weeds in the shallows. At one point Matt saw Don, through the green of his goggles, swim his awkward, overweight body down into a cluster of wavy plants and come out holding a jelly sandal. He held it up and did a funny underwater smile. Later, Matt found a dime placed perfectly on top of a rock. Don had a heart attack and died the next year, and Lucille sent him back, but at least Matt had the memory and, along with that, the very slightest notion that the earth could have its safe pockets.

He went into the bathroom to take a shower. For a long time he let the water run down onto the top of his head and down his back. Then, the other feeling strong, he looked at the white plastic showerhead and let the water spray him right in the eyes. He twisted it so the water moved to his neck, then, as an afterthought, he took hold of the showerhead and ripped it out of the wall with all his strength.

The tiles broke loose and clattered down to his feet as he continued ripping at the pipes. Water sprayed up onto the ceiling, and the crumbles of grout got down between his toes. He pulled more, silently watching the metal bend and new beams of water appear. At the edges of his vision, he saw a bright white. With one last yank, he pulled the pipes out all the way down to the handles and to the bathtub spigot at calf-level. He dropped them. He stepped out of the tub. He leaned down and turned the handles until the water was off, then reached to the wall for a towel and dried off.

II

O jungle

O jungle, are you anything but a provider
of contrast, of camouflage? The greens maddening
in the heat, the collective breath of frond
and orchid and spider. O jungle, are you anything
but a giver, a foe? Closely you gather your trees,
your species, and you eat them alive, you mark
their graves with flowers so terrible in their beauty,
the birds rattle in their hollow skeletons.
O jungle, you offer your regrets in your teeming
floor, your squawking quaking canopy; you tell us
it's a trade, that for this, blood for blood. O jungle,
you are the great interpreter of flesh, lover-true
in your patience.

— Renee Owen

9

"Is it big? Small? I'm still not getting a good picture."

"It's right in the middle. I'll send you a picture as soon as I find out how we can use email in this place."

"You know what I was thinking the other day?" Renee said. "I was thinking how unlike you this is. This is more like me. I'm supposed to be the klutz."

"Yeah, well," he said, "not this time."

Adam was wounded. What did wounded mean? Wounded meant he had tripped and fallen down a flight of stairs as he left a bar set up for soldiers in the Green Zone.

Why he was even allowed in and whether or not he had been drinking, Renee didn't know. She didn't care. He had broken his ankle and was in Germany now. His cast, according to him, was medium.

"You know, in some other time," she said, "this would be your ticket out of there."

"I didn't get drafted, Mom," he said. "I'm not looking for a ticket."

"I know, I know," she said. "But I knew people who found ways to hurt themselves to get out of the draft. Your father even had a friend who convinced the army doctors he was schizophrenic."

He didn't say anything. She should have known better than to bring up any of these stories with him. She knew he found them distasteful. She had found herself, though, in the last week, feeling a different kind of calm. Since Adam had his accident — it took a few moments of calm, deliberate explanation to a hysterical speakerphone audience of both her and Bill when he first explained it — a deep and nagging worry had been put on pause. It was a three-week window. He would have to go back, and he had many more months to serve, but for a few weeks she would be allowed to breathe and think of other things.

"I know you talk more to your father about these things," she said, "but he's out of town, so this time it'll have to be me."

"You're not about to give a sex talk."

"I'm only talking about what you *do*. With your days. What you did before you were hurt."

"You mean, when I'm in the field?"

"Yes," she said. "I guess."

"I thought you didn't want to know any of that stuff."

"I'm not sure whether I do or don't. There's some balance I need. I don't know."

"I can't really tell you anything anyway," he said. "It's okay, Mom. I'll be fine. It's a lot more dangerous in other places."

"Do you feel as though you've — you've learned things?"

"Learned things?"

"Whatever it was," she said. "What you wanted to know when you first decided to go."

Adam was quiet. Finally, he said, "I don't know. Some. Some good and some bad. I'll tell you more when I'm back, okay? I'm not really sure what I think."

"Okay," she said. "When you're back, I'd like to hear much more."

"All right, Mom. I'm gonna —"

"Wait, wait," she said. "Just wait. When you're back there, back in the war, will you just promise me that you're still doing whatever you think is right? Just promise me that you're still thinking, Addy?"

"Of course, Mom."

"But what I mean is that sometimes when you're there with many people, or when people have expectations for you, you think that means you have to stop thinking. Just promise me that you're still making choices, okay? Addy? That you still have your own sense of what's right and what's wrong. Not someone else's but your own?"

"I think I might get court-martialed for promising you that."

"You absolutely have the right to —"

"I was joking. Chill, Mom. I promise. I always do have that sense. And I won't stop thinking."

"Trust your instincts."

"Okay. I gotta go."

"I made them. I am responsible for those instincts."

"Okay, Mom. Good-bye. I love you. Tell Dad I'm fine."

"I love you, too."

She heard the click on his end. She pressed OFF and leaned

back into the wicker of the kitchen chair. Hand down on the table, she reached for her mug and slowly sipped at the rest of her tea. He sounded well. He wasn't home and he wasn't safe, but he sounded well, a third way that was the best she could hope for.

It was 7:30 in the morning. April 14. Bill was away in Miami for three more days. He was probably already at meetings, so she decided to call him later on. She had a reading to go to at nine anyway. So funny, the life of a children's author. Everything happened at the crack of dawn. The ghost of Truman Capote was only beginning to snort cocaine by the time most children's authors were finished with their social engagements.

Adam still didn't know; she and Bill had decided to wait to tell him. He was due back in July for leave, and they could tell him then — either that, or they could tell him later, when his tour was through. Whenever that would be. It was impossible to tell. She had chatted with many mothers whose sons had been sent back again and again. Renee just hoped it was late enough, that the feeling had turned so far against the war, soon it would be all but over. No winning, no losing. Just over.

As for Bill, his reaction to the news of her other son ("Well, where the fuck *is* he?") had been mixed. She had been right, at least, to think the news would hurt him. It did. Hawaii had been hard. In Hawaii Bill had, a few times, left her alone in the room and gone to the bar or taken walks alone. But he had come around, too. He had always known about Jonathan, this other love from the past. That wasn't the problem. Bill was an adult human being and knew that love happened more than once, at different times. The secret, though. Not telling. That was what hurt him. What he asked her, again and again, was this: have I ever done a thing to make you think I would not have understood?

That wasn't the point, as she had tried to tell him.

She roused herself, took a shower, dressed in what she'd laid out for herself on the bed. It was warm enough for a skirt — spring was coming through, stronger than expected, and outside the snow was gone and the grass was damp and breathing. She had another cup of tea, watched the news on the kitchen television, ate a banana, and left the house. She was annoyed about this reading, but the owner of Butterfly Books was a friend, and despite not having a new project to promote, she'd agreed. It was only just down the street. Afterward she was going to drive into the city and see her mother for lunch.

Adam didn't know. Bill knew. What about her? That question seemed to have no answer. The relief, after telling Bill, had been monumental. To think she would have gone her whole life and never said a thing. In a little more than one month she had become a changed person: lighter, freer. It seemed as though Bill was on his way to making peace with the news. So maybe those were the only questions for her: what do you think, what do you know, what do you want to know? She had accidentally taken amphetamines and had freed herself.

Waiting at a stoplight, she thought of the notebook stuffed in a drawer in her office. She had not read it over. She didn't know whether or not it was even legible. Her mind's eye, still in the office, turned to the bulletin board and to the white cards, now tacked in a different order altogether. She had made no progress.

She was twenty-five minutes early for the reading, and still Butterfly Books, only a few storefronts down from Dunkin' Donuts, was packed tight with children. Diane greeted her with a cry and a hug at the register. Another employee, Jane, came to chat. The children played together in the open space in front of the podium. Most of the parents mingled near the seats, sipping coffee, murmuring to one another, browsing, occasionally lifting their heads and focusing in on the swamp of moving limbs and screeches and saying things like "Do not. Do not. Do not. Do not. Do not. Do not. No. No. No. No. No. No. Put it down. Put it down. Good. Better. Put it all the way down, though" or "If you give it back to her, she will probably stop screaming" or "Your pants are missing" or "If you actually do eat that, Buddy, you'll get the runs." Renee's bad feeling about the reading fell away with all the energy. She loved this.

"Do you know what you'll be reading from?" Diane asked her. "We have everything out on the table there," she said, pointing.

"I thought maybe something from one of the Fiona and Samuel books?" she offered. "It's been so long since I've read from any of those."

"Oh goody," said the other woman, Jane. She clapped her hands together softly, up in front of her face. "I just love those books." She shook her head adoringly. "It's just so wonderful that you can come in and do this. For all these children."

"Oh, it's so easy," said Renee.

"I've written four or five books myself. Would you ever be able to read any of them?"

"Jane," said Diane, "that is what we call out-of-bounds. Remember?"

"It's fine," Renee said. To Jane, she said, "Actually, why not? I can probably read one. Just bring it in and I'll pick it up next time I come."

Jane, triumphant, turned to look at Diane.

"Yes," said Diane, "good work. But now you should go clean the bathrooms."

Jane, less triumphant, went to clean the bathrooms.

"Sorry," Diane said, leading Renee across the room to the table of books. "I knew she was going to do that. I've known since the day I hired her she was going to do that." Diane smiled. "Hiring is very difficult. You're such a star."

"It's fine," Renee said. "I will read it. Truly."

"That's nice of you, but you really don't want to. She has one with talking office supplies."

Renee picked the second Fiona and Samuel book, published in 1995. She ran her finger across the bright red cover. *The Case of the Upside-Down Man.* She remembered inventing most of the story at Adam's bedside. He'd read the first book and had asked her for more. The Upside-Down Man, a nice Southern gentleman named Mr. Grover Tillweed, woke up one morning with his feet attached to his wrists and his hands attached to his ankles and no idea how it could have happened. His only thought was to go to Fiona and Samuel, local amateur detectives, for assistance with his case. She opened the book to the middle of chapter one and read:

"I have heard you young Yankees do some special, special work in this town," Grover Tillweed said, adjusting his monocle with his shoe. "You see here now that my only inglorious choices are to walk on my hands or stand upside down like so. This is simply unacceptable for a man of my stature, children! I am confounded. Will you help? I can pay you for your services with either one bar of gold or one wish, magically contained within this cherry-wood box."

He reached up into his pant leg and produced the box in question. Fiona and Samuel discussed, then accepted.

"Yes, that one's fun," Diane said, nodding. "They'll love it. I wouldn't be surprised if they don't know it, too. There's nothing wrong with some restorying, right?"

"How long, do you think?" Renee asked.

"Oh, just twenty minutes should be fine," Diane said, flapping her hand. "Will you answer some questions afterwards?"

"Of course."

Diane quieted the children and introduced Renee. The children looked awed and clapped and yelled when Renee came to the podium. They had no idea who she was, probably. But she knew the amazement that was in their eyes: shock that a human being had done these things and existed and was here.

"Hello, children," Renee said, smiling out at them. "How are you all today?"

Screams.

Renee read happily through an early section of the book, even doing the Southern accent for Mr. Grover Tillweed. When she was through with the section, she took a sip of water and looked out at the crowd. She noticed him then. A boy — a teenager, though, not a child. He looked sixteen or seventeen. He caught her eye only because it was so strange to see someone his age here, now. Parents, yes; children, yes. Not this age. He wore a black sweatshirt and a gray winter cap and stood all the way at the back of the crowd, leaning against the windows. He had no expression on his face. Just a calm stare and dark eyes.

"Now on to the woods!" Renee said.

She read from chapter twelve and felt less comfortable. Fiona and Samuel had been trapped in a net, and she felt the children's concern — why was it that this empathy left our hearts, ever? — for their safety. She decided to skip the wolf and instead went on to the caves, which turned out to be less threatening. That was where they met the other brother and sister, the children in rags who had first gone out to simply hide but who had gotten lost and had now been alone in the forest for weeks.

At the end of the reading, she looked up, said, "Thank you," and smiled out at the applause. The dark boy was gone. The space where he'd been was back to only a window and the road.

"Now, children," Diane said, hustling up to the podium with her elbows out in a comic power walk. "*And* parents. I believe Ms. Owen will answer any questions you might have?"

Some children asked about the rest of the story. One girl asked for Renee's favorite color. One young father asked her whether she had any new books on the way, and if so, whether they could pre-order them. That got a nice chuckle.

Renee spotted one more hand in the back, a young woman wearing a bright pink sweater. Renee pointed, and the woman smiled nervously and said, "Hi, Ms. Owen. Um. My name's Tracey, mother of two. Okay. I teach Sunday school here in town, at St. Clement? I totally *love* this book and I love, just, all of your books. My kids love them, I read them when I was little, too. And so since I'm active in the church, my question is that I've always wanted to know whether you're a Christian, and whether the ideas in the books about good and evil and all that stuff come from, like, Christ?"

"Oh my, yes," Renee said immediately, answering this question for the thousandth time in her life. She had not been to church in forty-seven years. "I think you can absolutely say that they do.

Good and evil in all of my books would agree with almost any universal understanding of good and evil we humans have been able to come up with. That includes Christ."

Smiles.

The woman had a follow-up question. "Do you think you write the books so all those ideas — so children who read your books can learn those ideas and incorporate them into their lives? Or is it more just, like, a story? I guess what I'm asking is whether you think children's literature's central purpose is to teach?"

"I certainly want children to internalize these ideas," Renee said, nodding. "Ideas about more than good and evil, too. About fun, happiness, friendship, dignity, strength. Many different lessons, I think." She paused, thought. "I don't know about the central purpose," she continued, "and what it is when I write, but I know I want these things to come through."

Adam. She wrote the stories for Adam, of course. As another way of showing him what she thought about the world.

She waited silently and stared straight ahead. She looked at all the people in the crowd. She looked at Diane.

The woman nodded and seemed happy with the answer. A few other people raised their hands.

She had believed every word of praise, every review, every parent's note of thanks, as though she had . . . as though she'd actually meant to tell these things to the public, as though all along she had not been screaming these stories out. All the words weren't to make an army of children.

A man raised his hand and asked her whether she still wrote poetry, and who her favorite poet had been, and she said, "No." Then she said, "Walt Whitman."

Now the people in the crowd sensed something had gone

wrong. The children looked concerned. Renee tried to hold her smile in place. Not at all for an army. How could she have been this blind for this long? But that answer was simple, too. She had chosen to be.

Now a woman was asking a question. She was already asking a question. Had Diane called on her? She didn't see. Renee tried to focus in on the woman's mouth as she spoke. She was saying something about dragons. Renee nodded along as the woman spoke, and she even raised her eyebrows now and then at what seemed like the right moments. She tried to gather the question in. The woman wanted to know why children responded so well to stories that had, at one point in time, been the actual stories of cultures, the stories that adults told one another and that held the most meaning. Were thousand-year-old stories the hand-me-down stories children got once the adults had grown tired of them? Arthur, the Lady of the Lake — those had been serious business at one point in time, and the magic that drove the legends had been serious business, too. This was how people lived their lives. This was what they believed. Why, now, was this a game for toddlers? What had changed? Science? Maybe the industrial revolution had played a role. The woman revealed that she had a master's degree. Then she just said *Beowulf, Beowulf, Beowulf.* In Renee's ear the woman said *Beowulf* four hundred times in a row. Then the woman made a comment that made the rest of the parents chuckle, so Renee chuckled along with them. The woman apologized for rambling. She asked her question one last time. She said, "What I suppose I'm *really* asking is whether you see children's literature as an important aspect of our *culture* in, well, the same way that other *literatures* can be thought of as important? Should our universities' English departments be taking these books *seriously,* right alongside the traditional canon?

Right alongside Melville and Hawthorne, if you will?" and Renee leaned forward and said into the microphone, "I wrote every single one of these books for my son."

Jonathan died three weeks after he landed in Vietnam. He was incinerated. The image in her mind was almost a cartoon: a large round bomb landing directly on his head. That was her way not to imagine how horrible it had been.

She had started to read poetry before she met him, but something fused that fall, once she knew she was pregnant and once she knew he was dead. What poetry was seemed to change. It became more than what she was doing and far more than expressing. It became more like architecture of being. The poems she wrote for the book came that fall. Between October and December, she wrote one almost every day. To her it had been a curious, irrelevant coincidence that her teachers actually found what she wrote to be excellent. Most of the other undergraduates in class stared at her poems with confused looks and told her they liked the imagery. Either way, she just wrote. October to December, she wrote seventy-two poems, and her professor picked the best of them and collected them together into a folder and told her, "Just let me send these to somebody," and she agreed, and before Christmas she was told her book was to be published by a New York press. She just kept writing. Then her father gave her the Whitman, and she stopped.

It was important to remember the order. Wasn't it easy, after living fifty-eight years, to let one moment slip ahead or behind the other, and to make a new logic based on the new order? The usual order was this: he died, she had the baby, she gave him away, and then she stopped writing poems. Walt Whitman was only something in the background of it all. But that had not been the case. It was easy to put 1969 in that order, but the truth was she stopped writing before the baby, and before she gave it up. She stopped when she read that book. She used to read it in the park just down the road from her family's home, a brownstone on Racine. And her feeling, as she read those poems, was something like: if some other person from some other time has done exactly what I would most like to be able to do, then what is the point of doing it at all? It was already here. Someone had already brought it to earth. She knew that other artists felt this all the time, but she had not given up on the thought, and she had followed it to its logical end. She didn't need to write because everything she wanted written was already written.

It was not *Leaves of Grass*. It was not I am the grass and You are the grass and We are the Atoms and I am the dirt and We are lying beside one another but I am Myself and You are also Myself and I Touch Myself and look how it is both I and I here, on the Grass. All that meant nothing to her. The poems her father had given to her were other poems, smaller, kinder. They had less ambition. And in truth, it wasn't even the words, and it had nothing to do with what was described. It was something invisible behind them. It was tone, perhaps. It was voice. It was that when she read them she heard some other voice in her mind. When she read, "When I sitting heard the astronomer where he lectured with much applause in the lecture-room, how soon unaccountable I became tired and sick, till rising and gliding out I wander'd off by myself, in the mystical moist night-air, and from time to time, look'd up in perfect silence at the stars," she could hear someone saying it.

There she was, on the bench, a pregnant girl in Chicago with a voice of her own, but when she read the poems, some alien voice seemed instantly to be there within her, and the voice read the words back to her. It was not the voice of Walt Whitman. There she was, the girl reading the book, but someone else was speaking the words. How, though, could that have been? How could there be a voice that wasn't your voice? How could it be, unless this other voice was also your voice?

She stopped. There was nothing else to say.

Today was April 14, and Lake Michigan wasn't frozen anymore. There were no swimmers yet and she couldn't see any boats. It was the blue water and waves and the mucky, empty beaches.

People were here on the path. It was one of the first warm spring days, warm being over forty, and in the Midwest that meant wildly inappropriate clothing choices — it was as though they believed that if enough of them wore tank tops or shorts, the earth would think to itself that maybe its own orbital schedule was off and shrug and just decide to go right into summer. Renee had her coat, her hat, her scarf. Her mother, beside her in the wheel-chair, was also bundled up. She had a red checked blanket over her legs.

They moved north, with the water on their right. They had already eaten at a restaurant across the street from Theresa Owen's assisted-living apartment complex.

Renee tried to tell her mother what had happened at the reading and managed to say only some of it. Her mother already knew about Hawaii. Renee's mind was circling and doing some strange work of its own; it felt like she kept going down. The mood made it difficult for her to talk, and for long moments they just moved quietly together. She felt as though something beneath her, something in the floor, was gone.

"It's not all true, you know," her mother said. "You're a very good writer. Plenty of those stories have nothing at all to do with all that."

"With what? An abandoned boy?"

"Yes."

"They all do, Mom."

Theresa sighed and looked to the right, toward the lake. Her wheelchair veered right.

"Mom, look ahead. Just look straight ahead."

"I know, I know."

"You don't know."

Theresa piloted the wheelchair around the puddle.

"How well," Renee asked a few minutes later, "do you remember when I decided?"

"What? To give him up?" She frowned.

"I don't remember it at all," Renee lied. "Was it spring? Was it just before?"

"May. Sometime in May. Your father and I both came home and found you in tears. We said, 'What's wrong?' and you said, 'I can't.' And we took you to Evanston a week later."

Ahead on the left, Renee saw a young girl jog up to a pull-up bar, jog in place in front of it for a moment, then reach up and take hold of the metal. She was wearing a gray-and-yellow top, tight, and tight black running pants. Her hair was in a ponytail. For a moment the girl just hung, and Renee thought she might be stretching. Then she slowly lifted herself up, once, and slowly lowered herself back down. Again, she slowly lifted herself up, then she slowly lowered herself down.

"I'm not sure what to do," Renee said. "Now. This is — I think it's obvious that I can't go backward again. Or stay the same."

"Looking, finding," her mother said. "All very mysterious. Did I tell you about my keys?"

"No."

"Just last week. It was the strangest thing. I went down to eat and came back upstairs, and at my door I looked everywhere but I didn't have them. I went back down to the restaurant and asked them, and they didn't have them, either. I got the spare set from my neighbor, and she and I went over every single inch of the apartment. Nothing. I spent two days using the spare set, not having a clue. Do you want to know where they were?"

"It turned out you were wearing them."

Theresa frowned, looked down at her lap. She looked up. "Wearing them?"

"It's a joke."

"How would one be wearing keys?"

"You couldn't have been."

"If this were a story about glasses, I would understand the joke."

"I know, Mom. I see that."

"Your humor has always had this certain ... *confusion* to it."

"The keys, Mom."

"Yes, the keys," Theresa said. "Guess where they were? All along? You won't be able to."

"Where?"

Theresa smiled. "They were in Leipzig," she said. Her eyes glittered. "Germany!"

Renee looked down, waited. "Okay," she said.

"Isn't that amazing?" Theresa asked. "Isn't that just amazing? Halfway around the world!" She laughed again and shook her head.

Renee still waited.

"Well, how did they get there?" she said finally.

"I mailed them there," Theresa said. "I sent a book to Leslie Stewart at the University of Leipzig and I also dropped my keys into the box. I don't know how. I think maybe I tried to use one of the keys to cut the packing tape. We'll never know the secret. A few days later Leslie mailed them right back."

"I'm not sure," Renee said, "I understand the point of the story."

Theresa shook her head. "I'm not sure it has one," she said. "I just thought it was the strangest thing."

Renee pulled herself back together by the afternoon. She went home to her clean and very warm house in the suburbs and made toast and had a glass of wine. April 14. It was still only 3:30. She tried to watch television, but there was nothing on. There were two messages on the machine from Diane, both thanking her, both asking whether she was okay. Another from Bill.

Eventually she went upstairs to the office and stood in front of the board. She couldn't help herself. She had thought, a few times, of trying to use what she had written in the notebook, on the airplane, for the last poem.

Now that felt hollow. That had been her first attempt and it had not been right. It had just been more words, too many of them. All she was, was words. She couldn't just keep writing words. In the meantime actual life would be rolling on beneath her feet. She was so tired of all that kind of energy. Write that sentence and make sure the sun looks like it looks. What hand gesture would he make, really? Does the person telling it sound enough like a human being or is there too much there? Too little? Should she stand out of the way and simply let it happen? With children's books, tone was even more important. The whole idea of the world was in tone. Just a single word could change it, and the child-reader would be pushed out of the dream. She thought of the lifetime's energy she'd put into making those small choices. Each page of each book had hundreds of them. She thought of all the long days, locked in the office, coffee beside her, hunched forward and staring at the ever-evolving computer screens that had come and gone over the years. It was as though she'd been leaning forward and squinting at the light, hoping to see him inside the pages. Hoping that his actual human form could or would somehow materialize in some previously unnoticed depth a few hundred feet back behind the letters, and he would then step back and look around and see he was surrounded by them.

She looked at the dark monitor of the computer. Screen saver, stars. She heard the furnace all the way down in the basement creak to life.

The high-pitched pulse of the doorbell startled her.

She looked over her shoulder, then turned and went down the stairs, thinking it was probably Diane, here to check on her. She'd stayed with her in the back room at Butterfly, even though Renee had not told her what it was, exactly. She assured Diane it hadn't been any of the questions, it wasn't her fault. Only that she hadn't been right since Adam had left. Diane had made her a cup of tea.

The doorbell rang again when she was halfway across the living room, and she said, annoyed, "Hold on, hold on."

She turned the knob and pulled the door open.

She stood for a long time, looking at the boy — not boy, teenager — who stood in front of her.

Strands of his black hair peeked out from beneath his gray wool hat. He wasn't very tall — he was shorter than she. He had on a black sweatshirt and jeans, and his eyes were patient and calm but also piercing. She had seen him before.

"Hello," she said. "Can I help you?"

"You're Renee Owen, right?" he said. "I mean, I know you are. But I'm just asking anyway."

"Yes," she said.

"You don't know me at all," he said. "This is weird." He held out his hand. "I'm Joe."

10

It was early in the morning when Matt showed up at the house again, clean-shaven and rested. He'd ignored the mess of destruction in the bathtub when he'd stood at the sink with his razor and shaving cream, both bought at the drugstore down the road. He had the same clothes he'd been wearing since Thursday morning, but they weren't too ripe yet. They weren't not ripe, but they weren't too ripe. In the office, as he checked out, he told the man he'd slipped in the shower and had reached forward to hold himself up on the showerhead. Good enough. The man had stared back, unconvinced, and Matt had turned away from him.

At the front door, Darren's mother was also tidied up; Matt again thought of the masterful skill professional alcoholism required.

It was overcast today, not quite so orange and rosy. Matt sensed the air was pregnant with moisture, and above, the clouds slid by too quickly and too low, lurking and nearly apocalyptic in their altitude. Darren's mother looked better than she had last night.

She was dressed in some sort of business suit and had changed her hair; now it was down lower and wrapped around in a few perplexing knots at the back, which he saw when she turned to look over her shoulder after she opened the door.

"What did you decide?" she asked him when she looked back.

"This all seems very easy for you," he said, holding his hand out, palm down. "Slow down. I just want to talk."

"It's not that," she said. "It's that I knew you were coming." She smiled and showed Matt her yellow-stained teeth. They did not seem to fit properly with the rest of her.

"Right," he said.

"When all is said and done, Matt," she said, adopting a tone Matt found to be excessively familiar, "don't you think this is better?"

"I'm sorry. Do I know you personally?"

"No."

"You're talking like this has been an ongoing discussion."

"I've certainly had this discussion with myself," she said. "Although I don't think that's what you mean." She smiled. Had Matt not known any better, he would have said she was flirting with him. Her makeup now appeared cracked and grotesque on her cheeks and her forehead, and he could see the lines of age beneath the creams and the foundation. The mascara, too, was thick and gelatinous on her lashes.

"I met him last night," Matt said. "In his underwear."

"Well, that's absolutely irrelevant," she said. "He's always in his underwear."

"The point is, no, I don't think it's better. If you're asking me if I think it's better for him to live with me than you, then no. I am a stranger. You are trying to give me a child. In a different life where

I'd known him since the day he was born, and when Marissa had known him, maybe that would be better. Like this — this would not be better. This would only make it worse for him."

"Why are you here?"

"What?"

"Why are you here?"

"I'm here because I just found out my wife's mother had another baby."

"Is that all?"

"I also found out his father and his grandmother don't seem to give one shit one way or the other."

"But you didn't have to come," she said.

"Of course I did."

"No. You didn't. You found what you were looking for at Darren's house." She nodded over his shoulder, toward his truck. The cradle was strapped in the front seat. He looked at it, too, then turned back to her. He didn't recall telling her about it yesterday evening.

"You could have gone directly home and never said a thing to her," she continued. "That's not lost on you. Don't pretend it is — I can tell you notice these things. It's not lost on me."

"I didn't have to go get the cradle, either," he said.

"But you did anyway," she said, smiling. "See?"

"No."

"See?"

"How do you know this?"

"My psychic is very good."

"You've been talking to your son on the phone."

"Not true," she said. "I'm sorry to say that my son and I neither talk nor correspond."

"What you're talking about now," he said, "me driving away from here with a boy and bringing him back to my family — it's not the same. What about the documentation? What about the law? What about Darren? This is not pickles. This is not a cradle. This is a life. This is a human life that's going to go on for years. And remember everything. You can't just pick up a kid and walk away with him."

"You can if nobody wants him."

Matt's look was grim as he stood on the doorstep, watching her. She was very casual. He felt like stepping back and slamming the door in her face. She looked as though — well, as though she had known he was coming.

"Why don't you come inside," she said, "and have some cereal?"

"I want you to tell me when you plan to enroll that boy in school."

She raised her eyebrows, tilted her head, and stepped back into the house. For a moment he thought again of walking away.

He followed her in.

When they came around the corner, he saw that the boy, Joe, was at the kitchen table, dressed now and eating cereal himself. Beside his chair was a small suitcase and a colorful *Little Mermaid* backpack stuffed to the gills. He didn't look up; instead he stared down at his Life cereal and slurped at it from time to time.

"What is this?"

"This is Joe eating."

"Why is he packed?"

The woman just rolled her eyes.

"I haven't agreed to anything, lady. I can't take him. You have a family. I have a family."

She nodded, then went to the fridge and took out a sandwich

wrapped in plastic, then crossed the room and put it into her purse. "I'm sorry. I have to go."

"You have to *go*?"

"I have to go to church," she said. "You can let yourselves out."

"Lady," said Matt, "you are the absolute —"

"Good-bye, Matt," she said. She looked at Joe sitting at the table. "Good-bye, Joe," she said. Not even a touch on the shoulder and a squeeze.

"I could be anyone," Matt said. "And you're leaving me with him."

"We keep going around and around with this," she said. "You aren't just anyone. That's the point."

"If you go," Matt said, "I will call the police on you."

She ignored this and strode past them both and disappeared around the corner. Matt heard the door open and close, then he heard the engine starting.

Matt looked at Joe, who kept eating his Life.

"Is she always like that?" he asked the boy.

Joe didn't look up. Matt came across the kitchen and sat down at the table. He opened his mouth to speak again, but as he did, Joe snapped a hand forward to the box of cereal and filled the bowl again. He put the box down and crossed the room — he was wearing pants now — and at the fridge he got the milk and carried the big gallon container back to the table. Matt watched him pour by levering the milk slowly, standing on top of his chair. "You got it?" he asked, holding a hand in the general vicinity, waiting for a milk explosion. Joe didn't look at him or say anything; instead he kept a careful eye on the pour of the milk, then levered the jug back upright when he was through and popped the blue cap back on.

"Wait here, okay?" Matt said.

Joe started shoveling the cereal into his mouth. Matt doubted he was going anywhere.

He went into the living room and found the cordless phone. He poked his head in the kitchen to make sure the kid was still at the table, then went back into the living room and sat down on the sofa. He dialed home. Marissa answered after a few rings.

"Hey."

"Hey," he said. "I've got it."

"You've got it!" she cried.

"I've also got something else."

"You've also got something else!" she cried. "What? I'm the one who's supposed to have the surprise for you."

"I know that you said you didn't want to know," Matt said. "About anything. About where she was or what she'd done since then."

"I don't." Now she was less excited.

"I have to tell you."

"No, you don't," she said.

"No, Marissa," he said. "I have to tell you."

"You don't *have* to do anything."

"It's too important. Your little magical-quest idea has to end."

There was a long pause on the other end of the line. Then Marissa said, "I guess you're the one who has to decide."

"Decide what?"

"What's too important. For my magical-quest idea."

"I'm deciding, then," Matt said. "Hold on." He stood up, looked again at Joe, then walked past him, through the back door and out into the yard. He slid the door closed.

"I'm in Indiana. Your mother had another child a few years

after she walked out on you. An old woman who doesn't want him just gave him to me."

Matt tried to imagine the course of Marissa's thoughts after he said it. Most times he was wrong when he tried to predict the paths in her mind — she seemed to have an unpredictable sense of direction when it came to thinking. You could be talking about peanut butter and jelly sandwiches with her, wait ten seconds, and she would turn and ask you whether you had ever been to Kansas. And there was some sort of reasoning, some chain that led her from this to that. Now, as he waited, he thought that maybe the paths were leading her down to the night her mother had come home, then past that to a picture of the cradle in the sanctuary she'd found for it. Then past that to other places, dark grottoes where her mother slept with strange men, or past that and into sterile rooms where the women screamed in the throes of labor. Perhaps there was war, too. Perhaps she found herself all the way back, at Gettysburg, the cradle in the center of the battlefield as both armies, insectlike, converged.

"What does 'gave him to you' mean?" she said. "Where is my mother, Matt?"

"She's not here," Matt said. "She left. Again. She must have had him...a few years after she left you and Glen."

Marissa thought a little more, and again Matt waited.

"So who has this boy been living with?"

"With the father, for a time," Matt said. "Then he gave him away to his mother."

"Why do you keep using the word *gave?*"

"Because that's what all these people have been doing," he said. "I'm in some other goddamned dimension."

Matt looked back through the glass doors. Joe looked up at him for a moment, then returned to the cereal.

"He looks like you," he said to Marissa.

"Oh Jesus Christ, Matt," she said. He could hear that she was crying. "Don't."

"I'm sorry," Matt said, "but he does."

"That bitch. That *bitch.*"

"Mare."

He heard sniffling. She didn't bother to take the phone away from her face when she blew her nose loudly. Matt held the phone away from his ear, thinking that the snot might come through the holes.

"Matthew," she said, "why are you standing around in Indiana?"

"Because I'm —"

"You get him," Marissa said. "You get that boy, you put him in your car, you get his things, and you bring him home to me."

Don and Lucille Kincaid had not been angels, mind you. Matt remembered swimming in the lake and the songs, but there was another story from that time. As the bad stories of his childhood went, it was not particularly horrible, but it was one that had stayed with him more than the others, probably because his time with them was so mixed, so equivocated. Once, they'd left him at the house. For a vacation. Lucille had sat down with him at the kitchen table and had given him a long list of chores to do. She told him that he was not allowed to leave the house, and was not allowed to call anyone, and was not allowed to answer the door if it rang, and was to do his chores and read his books and play and they'd be back in four days. She showed him all the food and the cereal and she showed him the sandwiches in the fridge for him, each one marked for a particular day. She said, "You're a big boy now and you can do this on your own." Sometimes, now, as an adult, Matt wondered whether Lucille had been insane. Once, he found her standing in her bedroom, dressed up in one of Don's business suits, holding his briefcase and looking at herself in the mirror. She'd shooed him out. Another time she served him a salad with piles of ranch dressing. When he got to the bottom, he realized that in among the lettuce there were clippings of grass, too. She smiled and told him that she'd gotten them from the big bag attached to the lawn mower and had put a bowl in the fridge. "Just to try," she'd said.

He didn't wonder. Lucille had been insane.

What he couldn't figure out was why Don, too, had been so okay with leaving him for that vacation. No one was that stupid. Was anyone that stupid? Matt supposed it was too complicated and not something he could understand by tracing through his memories alone. That would require Don back alive, explaining. Whatever the reason, however, they said good-bye to him in the front room, patted him on the shoulder, and walked out with their luggage. He remembered the feeling of watching from the living room window as they pulled out of the driveway. Excitement. Then. Only later, on the second night, after the nightmares and a long thunderstorm, was it simple dread.

His dread took the form of tigers for those next days. He had hours and hours to envision their plans for him and to work out their exact paths as they circled the yard and slowly closed the noose. First they were up in the trees only — he saw them through the windows, saw the beads of their eyes glowing. Then they were more aggressive. They would come to the windows and stand all the way up, like cats, their great paws on the windowsills, their breath steaming the glass with a low purr-grumble. They even tried to break in through the door, but Matt had buttressed it with furniture and had stayed awake all night, in the center of the dining room, sitting upright on the table, twisting and making sure that every single sound he heard was something that he understood.

Matt had to move the cradle. Joe couldn't fit inside the truck with him if it was there as well. He had some bungee cords and a tarp in his utility box, so he removed the cradle, wrapped it, and tied it down as best he could. Not satisfied, he went into the garage of the house through the kitchen and found some twine, then used that to tie the cradle down better. As he worked, Joe followed him. First outside to see the cradle removed, then into the garage for the twine, then back outside. Matt didn't talk to him as he worked, but he was glad to see that the boy appeared to have a mind.

"Okay," Matt said once he'd tied the last knot. He looked down at Joe. "I think it's safe." He turned back and gave the cradle a few tugs. "You?" he said. "You think that's safe in there?"

Joe didn't say anything.

"You wanna see?"

Still nothing. Matt squatted down in front of him. "You've been moving around a lot," he said, and the boy kept his eyes focused on Matt as he talked. "One more time, then you'll be through. I saw you were all packed up."

Joe looked over his shoulder, back at the house.

"I have to ask you, though," Matt said. "Do you want to stay here? With your grandma?"

Joe looked back at him and didn't nod or shake his head.

"You don't know who I am," Matt said. "But we're related,

actually. You see, you've got a big sister. She's a lot older than you. She lives in St. Helens, which isn't very far from here. And I'm married to her."

Joe looked back at the house again.

"Your grandma talked to me for a little while and she said that she thinks you might have a better time coming to live with us for a little while. What do you think of that? Do you want to stay living here with your grandma? Or do you think you might want to meet your big sister?"

Finally, Joe shrugged.

"You don't know or you don't care?"

"I don't know," Joe said.

Matt smiled. It was the first time he'd heard a word from him. He said, "Okay. Well, what about this: how about you come to meet her, and you stay for a week or so, then we talk about it again and see what you want to do?"

Joe walked past him to the truck and looked at the twine that was visible from down below.

"I moved it to make space," he said. "So you can ride in the front. The cradle, I mean."

Joe looked at the truck.

"You like driving?"

Joe, still looking at the truck, started shaking his head slightly.

"No? I drive safe, mind you."

Matt stood and went back into the house, and Joe followed him in. They went to the kitchen and Matt leaned down and picked up the boy's small suitcase. Then Joe got his backpack. He spent a moment twisting his arms so it fit onto his back, then waited.

"Let me ask you a question," Matt said to him. "What's your favorite color?"

"Red."

Matt said, "Okay. Come on."

So this was happening. What it meant, Matt didn't want to think about. But it was happening. He was tired from the driving, from the questions, from having to tell his story over and over again. And yet somehow, here he was, with a cradle. And then some. Joe followed him out to the truck, and Matt opened the door for him and stepped back. He didn't know whether or not the boy would be able to climb in on his own, whether or not he'd have to lean down and hoist him up. But Joe didn't have much of a problem. He looked around the truck a little, then found a handhold, got a foot up, and hauled himself in, then climbed onto the seat and began arranging himself. "Good work," Matt said, and he leaned over and stuffed the suitcase behind the seat.

He went around the front, climbed in, started the engine, and looked down at Joe. "You ready?" Matt said. Joe didn't say anything. He was still wearing his backpack, and the hump of it forced him to lean forward a little bit in his seat. Matt looked closer and saw that he had peed in his pants.

"I guess we shoulda stopped in the bathroom on our way out," Matt said to him.

Matt hoped he would smile, but he saw that Joe's hands were shaking. He was staring straight ahead, into the latch on the glove box.

"Hey," Matt said, touching his shoulder. "Hey. It's okay." Joe just shook.

Matt turned the engine off, got out, and came around to Joe's side and pulled open the door. "Let's just do a quick changearoo and start again. For the first time. Sound okay?" He reached back behind Joe and got the suitcase, laid it on the ground, and sorted through the messy pile of clothes inside. He found a second tiny pair of sweatpants and held them up. "How do these look?"

Joe looked down at the pants.

"Okay, then," Matt said. "And also, we'll be needing one nice pair of Spider-Man underpants. Wouldn't you know it?"

Matt held up a pair of Spider-Man underpants.

"Okay," said Matt. "Hop out."

Joe started to climb down. Matt said, "Hold on. Leave your backpack up there." Arms rolling and body squirming, Joe slid out of the backpack, climbed down to the floor, and jumped out onto the driveway. He stood in front of Matt, and Matt started unlacing his sneakers. The pungent smell of urine wafted directly into his face. He said, "You know how to tie these things already?" He didn't bother looking up for a response.

Joe's shoes off, Matt helped him out of the sullied sweatpants, then helped him out of his white briefs, stained bright yellow, when Joe didn't start doing so himself. He couldn't help but see the boy's small penis. He didn't want to see it. Matt looked down. He picked up the Spider-Man underpants and held them open low and told Joe to step into them. The boy did, one foot at a time, and Matt pulled them up and let the elastic snap closed, then they did the same with the pants. Matt found a plastic bag in the truck and put the wet pants and undies into it, tied it off, loaded the suitcase back behind the seat, and nodded at Joe to climb up again. "Let's try this again, shall we?" he said.

Joe climbed in, this time quicker than he had before. Matt helped him set the backpack down on the floor, then closed the door.

He checked the cradle one last time in the back, then came around and climbed inside. He started the engine, put the truck into reverse, and smiled down at Joe. He shook his head with the smile to make sure it seemed like it didn't matter. "You ready to —"

Matt frowned.

There was a new stain in the crotch of the pants, right where Joe had peed again.

It took four stops and all of Joe's pants to get them out of Indiana. When they were through Chicago, Matt kept telling himself to just not look down at him anymore. He hadn't said another word or made a sound at all, but the shakes were coming intermittently. He was terrified.

That was what *alone* did. His fear made Matt again wonder at the wisdom of what he was doing. This was all too rushed. There had to be social workers involved, forms, consultations. A lot of bureaucracy. You don't just walk in somewhere and take somebody because he's given to you. A week ago none of this existed — not the idea to find the cradle, not wrinkled old women in Green Bay, not Darren, not Rensselaer, not the boy. Now it was impossible to back away from it. No matter what happened, it would be impossible to walk away from it.

He'd been numb since the woman had walked out of the house and had left him alone with Joe. He hadn't felt a thing. Now, though, beyond the frustration with the kid, as the highway past Chicago opened up, something was growing again. Something that was made by the Kincaids, in their way, but made more by all the rest. By the worst of them: by Clyde Hancock and his drunk German wife, Hilda, and by Mr. Wasserstein, and by the man whose name he'd never known, the janitor at the Fryer Boys' Home. He remembered this kind of fear now.

It wasn't fear, actually. It was dread. The hollow, stultifying pressure of it, the way it soaked into you and made something as simple as opening your eyes in the morning, realizing a new day was there for you, almost impossible.

He had scrubbed himself clean of it. He had literally spent years tearing out his own insides, all of his twenties spent removing everything that had come before, all of those years to remove each and every organ capable of producing that sensation of the past. He had known that if he didn't, he would always be followed by it. What had scared him even more, then, was giving it to somebody else, either passing it down to a child or transferring it sideways, to someone he loved, if he ever found somebody to love. He had, of course, and by that time he had taken the steel wool to the farthest edges of his mind and his heart and had left nothing unsterilized. All that was so far behind him... he had even taken care to scrub away the scrubbing itself, to mute it and make it small and make it seem as though it hadn't happened, hadn't taken every ounce of energy he had.

Tigers. Joe was sitting beside him, quiet. Was it not obvious then, what this other feeling was, this mysterious feeling of gratitude for a day? It was the same shape, just the opposite. He hadn't invented it himself and he had not been touched by the hand of God and granted a new emotion for doing nothing. No. That feeling that sometimes overcame him — that feeling that was coming again now and that was making his heart beat faster, making him start to sweat, making his hands shake a little — that feeling was what happened when he rushed through the carved passages of all that old pain, but rushed through them without the pain. Instead just existed and allowed himself to be what he was and what he had been at the same time. The divots and the paths and the channels that were there inside him were not malleable. Rather, it was what ran through them that was malleable.

He started pulling over. It was one of those. The sky in front of him was a pale blue and closing down in a circle. The edges, again, were turning bright white. What he was feeling now was both sides of it, he realized, reaching forward and sliding the gear-shift into park. The rage was nearly unbearable, but the joy, too, had mixed with it. Why, he didn't know. He hadn't the faintest idea what to do or say. This boy right here beside me, he thought. This boy. He looked over. Joe looked calm. He didn't have the faintest idea.

Matt got out of the car and leaned against the grill. It was hot, and he closed his eyes and let the feeling deep into the small of his back. He was an hour from home. But he couldn't go there. Not yet. That was the point.

Alone. This is what *alone* did. And to think there were reasons for it to happen, that it didn't just drop down onto you. That was what he hadn't understood when he was a child. That the world never just happened but rather was made by people, each and every aspect of it. Whether or not you could control it was beyond the point. It was not the question if you were a child. When you were a child, you couldn't control anything. That's what being a child was.

Later, though. Later, it was different.

What he felt he knew for certain was that without going, it wouldn't be secure. Without actually making it clear what would happen, and making sure the law was on their side as well, something could always go wrong. Someone could go. Someone could come back. Someone would change their mind. Matt knew, though, that he wouldn't change his mind once he decided. And actually, hell, he had already decided. So he would have to go back and make it clear, what he planned.

He found a phone at a gas station just a few miles down the road. He was glad that she didn't answer, and he left a message after hearing himself say that no one was home.

"It's Matt," he said. "He's here with me. We'll be home tomorrow. One more thing to do."

11

It was evening by the time they arrived back in Walton. The sun
was low in the sky, directly in front of the truck, slamming Matt's
eyes a little — his eyes itched, and he wondered whether eyeballs
could get burned — but despite its orange, the flatlands of southern Minnesota still looked gray. No matter how you lit it, barren
was barren, sterile was sterile. They'd stopped once to eat, and
now Joe was sleeping, curled up into a ball with his *Little Mermaid* backpack as a pillow. He'd had one more accident during
the drive. Out of clothes, they'd stopped at a Target in Madison
and Matt had bought three more pairs of little sweatpants for him
and a new package of underwear. He'd also bought a package of
Hanes white T-top shirts for himself in the spirit of hygiene. In the
checkout line, he'd seen a superbouncy ball, swirled in color, so
he'd also gotten that and given it to the boy.

This time there would not be any circling through the streets.
They passed the great dead mechanical beast and entered town
slowly. It was two nights ago that Matt had come here for the first

time. Now, though, it was different. All through the drive, he'd been carrying along the pulsing feeling that had overwhelmed him in Milwaukee. As they'd passed the St. Helens exit, he had stared straight ahead and had talked to Joe about the big icicles he remembered forming on the roof of the Kincaids' house, and how he'd loved nothing more than to throw snowballs at them and knock them down and then take them up and play with them like they were swords. There was something to the many steps of this game that he had loved. As he spoke, the urge to have what he was thinking to himself as a discussion with Darren Roberts tickled inside his limbs.

Just a discussion.

They passed the bank where Matt had withdrawn the money, then turned, then turned onto Darren's street.

Joe was waking up, and Matt said quietly, "We're here." As they passed Darren's house, Joe straightened up, and Matt wondered whether or not Joe remembered this town or this street. Probably not. The boy's mind was an opaque mystery to him. It wasn't only the not talking, it was everything else — the way his eyes moved with intelligence, the way his lips stayed still, never pursed, never changed position. He didn't smile, either. He only looked.

Now, he was looking out the window. He didn't seem very interested in Walton, or the street, or whatever memories were left.

Matt parked halfway down the block and turned off the car.

"Joe," Matt said, "I have a question for you. Actually, it's more of a favor."

Joe looked up at him.

"I have to run in and talk to a man in one of these houses," he said, waving his finger across the street. "I was hoping that while I'm gone, you could wait here and wear my hat for me."

His eyes ticked up to the hat on Matt's head.

"If someone doesn't wear it, then it gets less powerful. So I need it to stay on someone's head, and I can't wear it in there. There's something about that place that makes it not work. There's a person in there whose powers cancel it out."

Joe took in the baseball cap for a long time. When his eyes finally came back down, Matt said, "Okay?"

Joe nodded.

Matt took the hat off and dropped it down onto the boy's head. It was much too big, and the brim dropped down to cover his whole face.

"I just have to talk to someone for about ten minutes." Matt helped him rearrange the hat so it stuck off to the side, and up. "Now don't try to mess with it or anything," he said. "I'll be right back. Don't go anywhere. Don't try to drive to California or anything like that. It would just be too ridiculous."

With that, he got out of the car and walked down the road to Darren's house, hands in his pockets. He climbed the stairs and knocked loudly several times. He heard the dog barking, then heard Darren tell it to shut up.

"Who is it?" he heard Darren yell through the door. He sounded far away.

"It's me," Matt said. "It's Matt."

"Who the fuck does that mean?"

"Matt," Matt said. "The cradle."

"Oh," Darren yelled. "You. Yes, you."

"Yes, me."

"I can't get to you," Darren yelled. "Just come in. I left it open for you."

The janitor at Fryer's, he had been a tiger. There wasn't any other way to think about him. Cold steel-blue eyes and his god-damned dry mop, always moving slowly up and down the halls, sweep by sweep. But he was hunting. He was crouched and hunting. Matt never saw him using any water on anything. Just the sweep-sweeping, glances here and there, passes in the hall in line with all the other boys. There was a bathroom in the lunch hall, but one day it was broken. It was early in his stay there and Matt didn't understand anything yet, so he'd asked the old man with the mustache and he'd patted him kindly on the shoulder and had told him where he could find the other bathroom, down the hall. Matt had hurried there, hands pressed down hard into the pockets of his jeans. Then inside, through the door, into the large tiled room, and there he was, leaning back against the windowsill on the far side of the room, smoking. The sweep-sweeper was beside him. He had brown hair with a violent strand of gray at the front, folded back and slicked. He was long and skinny, dressed up in an aqua-blue jumpsuit, and he didn't move when Matt came in. Matt stood still, dying to go to the bathroom, hands still thrust down in his pockets. He looked at the urinals. The janitor said, "Hey, fella. Just come in."

Matt pushed the door open and stepped into the house. He found Darren in the center of the living room, upside down, strapped in at the feet to a big metal frame.

Matt had seen commercials for the thing on late-night TV. Some yuppie exercise invention. It looked like a torture device.

Darren looked like a vampire bat at the moment. His hair hung down from his head and touched the floor. His arms were crossed at his chest. Darren the Dog was on his back, balls up, nearby.

"Hello there," Darren said, upside down as he was. "You seem to have come upon me in a compromising situation."

"Should I even ask 'What the fuck'?"

"Back strain," said Darren. He stretched his arms out. "Originally, mind you. During the course of my rehabilitation, I had a transcendental experience, however."

"You don't say."

"A lucky coincidence. I found that this kind of position also helped me to organize my thinking." Darren's hands were now up near his hips, and he squeezed two canvas straps. "Think of it as a focusing device. A kind of crystal that promotes deeper sorts of organization, et cetera."

"You look organized."

"You say that," Darren said, pointing. "You joke. But you know something? I knew you'd be back. So maybe you're not so funny after all."

"Maybe you should turn around," Matt said, "so we can talk."

"You mean right side up?"

"Whatever."

"Is he here?" Darren asked.

"Is who here?"

"My son."

Matt took another step into the room. He had parked far enough away, and he doubted Darren had seen them through the window. "No," he said.

"No?" Darren said, surprised, raising — lowering — his eyebrows. "Then I was wrong on that count. Sometimes I am, I admit it. Excuse me. I saw you as coming back with him. When I got the whole, kinda, idea of it."

"So you've been talking to your mother."

"Neither my mother —"

"Stop," Matt said.

Darren sighed. "You don't understand, do you? Not that I'm surprised. Nobody ever gets shit about shit when it comes to this. Both of us — we are special people. I don't know how else to say it. She has her way, and I have mine."

"That's not helpful."

"But we no longer talk," Darren continued. "Let's just skip it. I could tell you another long story, but fuck that, okay? Without getting into the specifics, Matt, you'll just have to accept it."

"It doesn't matter anyway," Matt said. "If you're so special, then you know why I'm here."

Darren closed his eyes then, nodded his head. Matt watched as his right hand released from the strap and moved right, through the air, and began feeling around near the table. The hand crawled around the table until it found a can of Miller Lite. Darren then brought the beer to his mouth and drank upside down. A good amount spilled up his face and dripped off his forehead onto the carpet.

After he put the beer back on the table, he said, "I do know why you're here. You're here because you want to keep him."

"I'm here for more than that," Matt said.

"What, then?"

"First of all," Matt said, "*keep* is not the word. *Give* and *keep* are not the words."

"What are the words, Matt?"

"I don't want to keep him. I want to give him a family so he doesn't have to be raised by some alcoholic woman who doesn't care one way or the other. Or you, for that matter."

"What am I?"

"What?"

"You described my mother with a high degree of accuracy," Darren said. "I'd like to hear you do me."

"By whatever it is that you are," Matt said. "Someone who doesn't care."

"It's outright impossible to burp when you're in this position."

"Then turn around and talk to me."

"I think I'll stay down here, thank you," Darren said. "And you're right, by the way. I don't care."

"So I want your word then," Matt said. "Your word that when all the papers come, you'll sign them and you'll send them back. It costs you nothing. You and I both know it's the best thing that could happen."

"Is it?" asked Darren. "For who? I also question your use of *best*."

"I don't," Matt said.

Darren smiled and blinked a few times as though he'd heard just what he'd been waiting for. He said, "This is the problem with all you people. You forget that *best* is an opinion no matter what."

"All what people?"

"I guess I just mean people."

"Think that if you want. In this case that's just not true," Matt said. "You know it. No matter how much you say you don't believe in anything."

Darren had no response.

"You're a person, I'm a person," Matt said.

Still Darren said nothing.

"There's more that I want from you," Matt continued. "Sign the papers. But something else, too."

"Yes," Darren said. "Go on. I'm very interested in your mortal plans."

"You'll never come looking for him," Matt said.

"Well, I can promise you I won't do that," Darren said. "Straight up, man. I told you."

"Most people I've ever known who pretend to be like you wake up one day and realize all along they just hate themselves," Matt said. "And that was the problem. So excuse me if I don't think you'll always be this way."

"Suit yourself," Darren said. He crossed his arms and closed his eyes again, and again he looked like a vampire bat. "But always have, always will."

"Beyond that, though," Matt said. "The more important part. If he comes to find you one day — and I'll do everything that I can to stop him from trying, I fucking promise you — but if he comes to find you one day, even though I tell him not to, even if I tell him that the last time I saw you, you were hanging upside down in your living room, telling me you didn't care one way or the other, and he shows up here, or wherever you are, you will act like you are gracious."

Darren's eyes opened. "That's wonderful, imagining me like that."

Matt waited.

Darren locked his fingers together, then cracked all his knuckles. The dog turned its head to look.

"Okay, then," Darren said. "Seeing as I have no reason to do any of these things, my response to you is simple, Matt. I'll do all of it. You just answer me my Question of the Ages. If I say your answer's good enough, then I give my word. If it's not good enough, then I won't do it."

"I am not answering a goddamned riddle," Matt said, "to decide whether or not he comes with me."

"You'll have —"

"Listen to me. Every single person I've talked to since I left my house has been absolutely out of their fucking minds, but listen to me, Darren, just actually listen to me: no matter what, he's a real boy. Joe is a real boy."

"Yes, he is," Darren said. "Youth."

"This is real."

"Yes. I believe that. I never said a thing about not believing that."

"So I'm not playing a game with you."

"No?" said Darren. "You won't play my game? Oh, painful to me. But don't you think I'm enough of a crazy sonofabitch to not do any of these things and send that little fucker, that real boy, to some real-ass foster home somewhere just because you wouldn't? Or, shit, you know what, Matt? Maybe I do want him after all. Maybe I have some things I wanna teach him about. So maybe he should just come back here. Maybe I'm ready. Maybe I've grown."

"No matter what you say," Matt said, "I know that you care, and that is why you'll do it. This is all real. His life is real. This is real."

"Answering my question is a lot better than me just shootin' you, isn't it?" Darren went on. "Then shoot myself for fun? Or, I don't know, eat you before I shoot myself? Or something? Because I could do that with equal nihilism. That's one of the wonderful aspects of my point of view, Matt. And let me tell you, you glowing uptight real motherfucker, in the last couple of days I had a lotta nice ideas, friend, but instead I decided to meditate and await your arrival this way, because I thought it might be more interesting, and because you've got something about you I like, and because, as you know, I am a student of the human condition."

"Okay," Matt said, "fine. Ask. Ask, and I'll say some answer, and then I'll go, and then you'll keep your promise. Because you give a fuck."

"No," Darren said, "I don't. The answer's gotta be good or you lose."

"You give a fuck," Matt continued. "You're alive and you're here, and you think it matters, and because saying it matters is just another way of saying you're alive and you're here."

Darren was silent for a long moment, frowning.

Then he said, "Huh."

"What?" Matt said.

"The strangest thing," Darren said. He shook his head once, violently, then put his pinkie into his ear. "Very strange."

"What?"

"No."

"No, what?"

"I'm not talking to you," Darren said. "Hold on."

Matt waited. Darren did a little sit-up then and loosened one of the boots holding him in. He put his arm on the ground, then reached up with his other hand and did the same again. Darren the Dog was up and excited, wagging his tail, and Darren shoved him away and lowered himself down onto his back and stood up right in front of Matt.

"Good-bye, then," he said, and he went past him to the door.

"What about all of that?" Matt said. "What about your Question of the Ages?"

Darren opened the door and looked outside, then turned back.

"I have determined that there might be some other goddamned paths," Darren said.

"Like what?"

"I just suddenly got in a bad mood," he said.

When Matt still looked confused, Darren pointed out the door and said, "Look. Send the mail here to the house. I didn't get to say it out loud. Maybe I'm not so smart after all."

They were ninety miles away when the radiator blew up. Joe had been sleeping since Matt had come back to the truck. When he'd come back, he'd found the boy shaking again, and it had taken him a few minutes to calm Joe down. Matt had said, "This isn't normal, all this driving. So this is the end. You don't have to worry about it. This was something else. Now we just have to drive a little more and then we're done. Keep the hat on."

Joe didn't wake up when the engine rattled, then popped, and the steam started shooting out. Matt pulled the truck over to the side of the road. Everything around was black. They'd crossed the Mississippi and had gone through La Crosse. As Matt sat, thinking, a semi blasted by. About a half mile back he had seen the sign for a campground, and he figured it was either find a phone somewhere and call a tow truck, get it towed, find some hotel, get it fixed, then go home, or sleep at the campground, try to get it fixed in the morning, and be home at the same time with a lot more money. He looked at the clock. It was 10:13. He closed his eyes and turned the key and promised his truck he'd do something nice for it so long as the engine didn't melt.

He did a U-turn, went back to the campground, and pulled off onto the dirt road. They trundled down it, slowly. There was no one at the entrance when they pulled up, but a light was on in a little cabin past the semaphore, and when Matt stopped, a teenager came out holding a can of Coke and walked up to the window and said, "Ten bucks for the night." Matt paid him, and the kid raised up the gate and waved him inside and told him, "C6," as he idled by. They drove down an even smaller road; here and there he could see tents pitched, and a few sites had campers in them. He found the Cs, and together they rolled into the empty patch of dirt. Matt put the truck in park, closed his eyes, leaned his head back. "Just for the night," he said.

Joe was sitting up now, and he looked back at Matt. "You want a Twinkie?" Matt said.

Joe nodded.

Matt reached into the glove compartment and found one of the two remaining Twinkies. He broke one open and handed it to Joe, then broke the other open for himself and started to eat it.

"Do you have a tent in that backpack?" he asked Joe.

Joe said, "No."

Matt looked at the big sodium light hanging above the bathrooms twenty feet away. "What we're gonna do," he said, digging around behind the seats, "is make you a little bed in here. So you can sleep right here and I'll sleep in the back of the truck. Right back there. Then it'll be morning and we can go home. What do you think of that plan?"

Joe kept looking down at the Twinkie.

"We don't have to do anything like this again," Matt said. "You'll actually get a room. You don't really have a lot of reason to believe me at this point. I realize that."

He found the fleece blanket he'd been looking for and laid it out.

"You thirsty?" he said. "I've got water. You have anything in there you haven't peed out?"

Joe shook his head, then slowly crawled himself into position and lay down across the seats. Matt helped him arrange his backpack up near his head so he could use it as a pillow.

"Both you and me stink, kid," Matt said. He reached down and touched Joe on his head. He scrabbled the hair around a little. "Showers for both of us tomorrow." He picked up Joe's dirty bag of clothes and shut the door.

The dumpster wasn't far away, and Matt tossed the bag into it and then came back to the truck and climbed into the pickup, slowly. Once he was all laid out, his head up just beneath the cradle, and everything was quiet, the everyday world moved aside like something was pushing from within. He waited and felt it. He pushed himself up a little closer to the cradle and closed his eyes. This was a onetime thing, all this driving. We don't have to do anything like this again. As though the world and the stars would never again offer up something that needed to be punished.

"I will kill you," the janitor had said to him many times, and each time he said it, another voice in Matt's head said back, No. Don't you see that I will be the one to kill you? But he'd never had his chance, had never been alone with him in the bathroom or the closet or the boiler room and happened upon the gun he always dreamed of holding or the razor he always dreamed of sliding across the man's half-shaved tiger neck.

Then one day the janitor quit, and there was a new one, a woman who never talked but who handed out caramel candies to the boys, especially if they didn't leave bad messes for her to deal with alone.

It was three months later that the letter arrived for Matt, with its cold computer-printed faded font, telling him there was a foster family named Kincaid who would be taking him. He didn't have any friends to say good-bye to and barely owned a thing.

Lying here in the bed of the truck reminded him of that night. That night he lay in his bunk, staring up at the wood frame of the bed above him, and listened to the sounds of boys whispering here and there; even, from time to time, some footsteps. But he didn't turn and look under Mr. Whittaker's door for the light to pop on. Instead he stared straight up at the crosses of wood keeping the other boy's weight from collapsing down onto him.

He remembered what he kept thinking that whole night. He remembered he just kept asking the same kind of question over and over again: why did you do this to me? Why did you do this to me? Why did you do this to me? Why did you do this to me? Why did you let me be here? Why did you make this choice?

Through the night Matt slept on and off, woken up by mosquitoes and once by the haunting sound of drunken laughter coming from somewhere else in the campground. The metal underneath him was painful, but he didn't want to sleep on the dirt. It seemed important to stay where he was. What dreams he had were of Lucille Kincaid trying to serve him grass. Once, she looked at him and said, "You don't have me because I am not your mother."

The stars were still visible when he woke after that, but the moon was gone, and he drifted away again. When he opened his eyes next, it was light and he was cold.

Joe had left the cab of the truck and was now sleeping beside him on the metal, curled up with his back against Matt's hip.

Matt reached down and touched the boy's head.

12

"We'll be home today," Matt said. "I just called work and told them I'd be in tomorrow." The radiator had a hairline crack, the mechanic had said, so he'd tried to seal it and they'd refilled the fluid. It would get them home, at the very least.

"What'd they say to that at Delco?"

"No one was happy. They'll be all right."

"Matthew," said Marissa, "where did you go? Why aren't you here?"

Matt stared at the wall of the truck stop. Joe was still inside the car, and Matt was leaning against the grill of his pickup, feet crossed, staring at the silver buttons on the pay phone.

He said, "It was just one more thing. I went to see his father and made sure he'd agree to it all."

"All the way back? Why didn't you leave him here? With us?"

"I just didn't want to keep droppin' him off to different people, Mare."

"Okay," she said. "Okay."

"We're gonna eat, then drive the rest of the way. We'll be there by one or two."

"How is he?"

"He's fine."

She paused, then said, "What's he like?"

"You'll have to meet him. He's quiet. He likes Life cereal. That's all I know."

"Is this too crazy?" she asked. "To do all of this? Tell me if this is too crazy, Matt. Talking to you yesterday, I just felt how right it was to have him come live with us. Now it's the next day and I'm thinking maybe it's not so right."

"There's nothing crazy about it at all," Matt said. "You felt right the first time."

"Daddy's all messed up," she said. "He's coming over later. He took the day off of work, too."

"Okay," Matt said. "We won't be long."

Inside, in a booth, Matt tried to quiz Joe about what he liked, but he wouldn't talk, and he only looked down at the menu. Matt realized he probably couldn't read. There were large, bright pictures of possible breakfasts. Joe was smiling at them.

"You like pancakes?" he said. "Everyone likes pancakes."

Joe shook his head no.

When the waitress came, Matt nodded to her and ordered an omelet. "And what would you like, darling?" she said, turning to Joe.

Joe looked up at her.

"Do you have cereal?" Matt asked her.

"We've got some Cheerios," she said.

Matt looked at Joe, eyebrows up. Joe nodded.

"Looks like we'll take one order of Cheerios."

When she left, Matt sipped at his coffee a little, then looked at

Joe and said, "I know you wanna talk. I'm not saying you have to. You don't have to do anything. I'm just saying that somewhere in there I bet you anything you've got a little ticker running and saying things to yourself. You know that everyone has that, right? So when you want to talk, what you do is you open up the door a little bit and let some of it run out to your mouth. Just be careful with what. Some people in the world just open the door completely and they never stop talking. You don't want to be like that."

Joe smiled even though he was looking down. He pulled the bouncy ball out of his pocket and stared at it.

"You don't wanna be the other way, though," Matt said. "And never do it. You need that, too. You need to talk to people. Everyone does."

Joe kept looking at the ball.

"There's a balance," Matt said.

He was going to leave it there, as Joe still hadn't looked him in the eye, but one more thought came to Matt's mind, and it was as though he had to say it, as though he was convinced by his own advice about letting some things out, about needing to sometimes allow the unexpected transmissions to break through. How else did one tell the truth, ever? Messages came up from all sorts of sources; at times they were not correct. He felt this one was.

He said, "You're free."

Joe looked up at him.

The boy's dark eyes were clear and unwavering.

Matt said, "Everyone's free."

They ate their breakfast in silence. He felt none of the mountain-moving feelings he'd felt in the past week and instead was just locked in a kind of easy, low feeling. He thought about Darren. He imagined him upside down in his machine. He hoped he'd never see him again or have to think of him again. He wanted him simply to be gone. He knew he probably wasn't, but for now he would allow himself to believe he was.

When they were finished eating, Matt said, "Okay. Now there's something important we have to do. No more talking, no more eating."

Joe was scooping around at the bottom of his cereal bowl.

"One minor pit stop down there," Matt said, nodding. "Come on."

He left money on the table and tried not to think of what he'd spent on gas and rooms. It would take months to get things stabilized again. He led Joe down the hall of the truck stop and then they came to the bathroom door. "This is what they call a public bathroom," Matt said. "Got it?" He pushed open the door.

Inside, Matt told him all there was to know about urinals, then demonstrated how one approached the urinal, used the urinal, flushed the urinal, and stepped back away from the urinal, then went to the sink, then went toward the door. He said, "That's the whole thing. It's easy. I'm sure you know about this. So think of all this as a refresher course."

Joe looked at the white urinal.

"Now you," Matt said.

He looked up at Matt.

"Really," he said. "It's easy."

Joe took a step forward, then slid the ball back into his pocket. He looked at Matt one more time, then walked the rest of the way, to the kiddie urinal, and stood in front of it.

"Don't forget the pants," Matt said.

Matt watched, pleased, as Joe went through all the steps. On the walk back out, he put his hand down on Joe's head again and said, "Good work," and they walked through the glass doors, into the sun. It was a beautiful day. People were moving about, gassing up their cars, sitting at picnic tables. Across the lot there were about twenty semis all in a row, and Matt could even see a few of the truckers through the windshields. He felt a strong, strong sensation of needing to be home. But they weren't far away. They went to the truck, and Matt said, "Okay. Last stop. You need anything else? Otherwise we're going straight through."

Joe shook his head no, and Matt nodded, opened the door, and helped him up into the truck. It was just as he was shutting the door that he looked to his left and saw that the cradle was gone.

Matt's eyes went wide, and he moved to the empty space. Bits of his twine were there but frayed, and the bungee cords were in a little twisted pile. His head shot up, and he looked back and forth at all the different vehicles and all the different people he'd just so sentimentally considered. He closed his eyes for a second, enraged, and mashed his teeth together. He should have parked somewhere where he could see the thing from their table, through the window. Why hadn't he?

"Please don't tell me you don't know that woman" came a man's voice from behind.

Matt turned. There was a yuppie-looking guy standing two spots down. He was at the trunk of his Volkswagen. "What woman?"

"Goddamnit," the man said, shaking his head. He closed the trunk, then stepped closer. "So I was standing right here, okay, and I watched this chick walk by, then walk by again. Then she came back and cut all of the string with a little knife and just picked up whatever that whole bundle was and walked off with it."

"When was this?"

"Ten minutes ago," he said. He shook his head and looked out at the highway in the distance. "I'm sorry, man. She drove off. I kept thinking it was shady, but I thought it was hers. Or her truck. Or something. I don't know."

"What'd she look like?"

"She wasn't too tall. Short. Red hair. Maybe fifty-five or sixty."

"You have got to be fucking kidding me," Matt said, crossing his arms and closing his eyes.

"What was it?"

Matt opened his eyes and looked at the man.

"What was what?"

"What'd she take? Under the tarp."

Matt looked back at the empty bed of the truck, then looked back at the man. "It was a cradle," he said. "From the Civil War."

The man nodded, put his hands on his hips. "Well," he said, "that totally sucks."

Matt didn't know what else to tell Joe just before he turned the engine off. He didn't say anything to the boy. Instead, he looked down at his knuckles.

Joe was transfixed by the front of the house. Matt was impressed: Joe was probably the first person in the history of St. Helens to be transfixed by the front of this particular house. It was yellow with white shutters and a tar-paper roof. The front porch and steps were concrete, and a long crack ran along the stairs. It had been only getting bigger. There were weeds here and there, but the lawn looked okay still, even though he hadn't mowed since last week, since before the barbecue. They were home.

Matt opened his mouth to just say "Okay" to Joe, but as he did, he looked up, and Marissa opened the front door of the house and stepped out onto the porch, arms crossed, and then Glen, behind her, floated, looking furtive.

Marissa's hair was gone. She'd cut it all off again. Now it was cropped short, a little bit spiky here and there. Matt smiled and she waved, but she waited there on the porch.

He'd given Joe their names and had tried to explain again who they were. What else could he do? He leaned over and said, "Okay," then opened his door and got out. He went to Marissa and gave her a long hug, pushing his cheek into her neck and breathing in. Her belly pressed into his.

He said, "Hi," and she said, "Hi."

"Why'd you chop it off?" he asked her. "I was starting to get used to you being stylish."

"Every single thing is uncomfortable," she said. "I had to do something. It was pretty much all I had left."

He put his hand in her hair and scratched her head. "It looks good."

Matt turned to Glen and held out his hand to shake. Glen took it and shook it but didn't look at Matt.

He was still looking at the truck.

"His name's Joe," Matt said, turning and going back to the truck. Before he got there, Joe had already opened the door, and Matt took his backpack and helped him get down.

Matt closed the door and Joe stood quietly, looking at Marissa and Glen.

Marissa took a few slow steps forward, then squatted down low and said, "Hi, Joe," and waved from across the yard.

Glen was still up at the door. Matt saw that he'd turned another color, something whitish-green, and he was backing away, into the house.

"Daddy," Marissa said, looking back over her shoulder, "stop blubbering. Go get him his present."

Glen backed all the way in and disappeared.

Marissa stood up. Matt put his hand down on Joe's head and they walked a little closer to the house. "So this is where we live," he said. "It's small, but there's enough room for you to stay. You want to come inside?"

Joe looked up at him, considering. He looked back at Marissa. Matt could see that he had the shakes, but only a little bit.

Glen reappeared in the doorway, holding a white box with a red bow on it. He paused for a moment, then walked down the stairs and came out, past Marissa. He squatted down then, in front of Joe. Matt saw the bottom of his jaw quivering, and his lips stretched back and his forehead crinkled and he started to cry a little bit. Glen. That was him. What it could have meant to see this boy, Matt didn't even dare guess. He watched Glen's ragged face turn up into whatever smile he could manage. He said, "Joe, we got this for you." He held out the box of Life cereal. "We have different kinds of milk. So whatever you'd like to have."

Joe took the box.

Glen stood, turned, and walked back into the house.

13

She remembered it.

Renee was lying to her mother when she told her she didn't remember the day. The day she decided. That was a better way to say it, too. Not repressing. Lying, not repressing.

It was May 17, 1969, and the baby was due in a month. Her stomach was enormous. Both parents were tied down at school with the end of the term, and she had free rein over the house. She was already depressed, but that day, the feeling — she didn't know if it was grief or anticipation — was different. It was heavier and more destructive.

She read for an hour in her bedroom, then went downstairs. Sitting alone in the kitchen, she thought about how the baby, if it was a boy, would look like Jonathan. This thought sent her mind wandering down familiar paths — not just that she was afraid one day she'd look at him and see Jonathan and it would simply be too painful, but that other pains, more abstract pains, were possible. For example, say he one day grew up and went to war and died at war, too. Then it wouldn't just be that someone who looked like Jonathan haunted her life every day. It would be that it had all happened again, in one big circle. That the same man she loved had died twice.

That day she left her parents' house and walked down to the corner, to the drugstore. She wandered up and down the aisles, not looking for anything, just taking in all the packages, the reds and whites and greens, the brown bottles, the clean tiled floor. In the neighborhood these days, she had become something. All the local people saw her walking up and down the streets or saw her sitting alone in the park, reading her Whitman, and they all knew her story, and they pitied her. She had felt them watching for months, and she felt it now, too, here in the store. Mr. Henshaw, standing behind the counter, smiled at her when she walked by. His mustache wrinkled into an M. She smiled back and she thought: don't pity me, you old bastard.

She left the drugstore and went across the road to the very park where she'd first read the Whitman, and she sat on the bench, holding her stomach, both feet flat on the ground, watching children play in the field. She watched the six of them play football for what must have been an hour. One boy — angry, gaunt, brown-haired, and ugly — seemed older than the rest, and he played with a frenzied enthusiasm his teammates didn't share. Renee, a few times, wondered where the parents were. No one else seemed to be around. The children never talked to her or gave any indication that they noticed her. They just kept playing. There was only one girl. After a time Renee guessed that her brother was the ugly one. She seemed to play with passion, too, and the few times she stumbled or dropped the ball, she said nothing; she just stood and walked back to her team and started over again. Another boy, the smallest of the group, got hurt. He twisted his ankle and started to cry. It was enough of a problem to send one of the other children running away, and Renee watched the injured boy intently, sitting on the ground, bawling, looking at his foot. No parents came. She stood up and left the park.

She was them. That was the deepest truth. Children played a game, and their whole world was caught up inside it, the whole range of happiness and sadness. There was absolutely nothing outside their own world, and that's what let them be what they were. And she knew, walking home, that if she had to choose, if she had to say I am this or I am that, I am those children playing in the grass, or I am my parents, or I am all the other people in the world, I am them. I am the children playing in the grass. I am not some other thing. And if she was that, how could she have a child of her own?

Joe Bishop first told her about the fire at Delco. Nineteen people had died, another sixty-seven were injured. An ammonia compressor exploded in the southwest wing at 9:15 in the morning, after the shifts changed. Four men and one woman died there, in the explosion. It took almost no time for the holding tanks to catch, and even though the sprinklers were spraying full bore, even though the fire trucks had arrived, there were explosions up and down the floor as though it were a war. Joe said the shift boss, a man named Gary Pollian, was trapped inside his office and tried to call his family on the phone before he burned to death. Matt's friend Eric Granderson had died, too, but he had died of smoke inhalation, and his body had been found without a mark on it. Since January there had been new investigations — they said the safety measures had not been up to code, that it wouldn't have happened at all had the water dump worked or had the insulation around the tanks been re-fireproofed sometime in the last thirty years. It was possible there would be a class-action lawsuit. Joe said that at the very least, there were many, many people in St. Helens without work. There were many mourners and many people without work.

Matt had survived. His arms and hands, though, had been burned from reaching through a hole in the wall, trying to help a man climb through. Apparently just as Matt reached back, there was an explosion on the other side of the wall. The force of air that came through the hole knocked him twenty feet, and he landed in a wide-open space in the center of the main floor, stood up, looked back to where the hole had been, to what was now a flaming wall, and ran out of the plant with a group of other men. It was only after he was outside and safe that he realized his hands and forearms were different colors.

That was the first story. Renee listened to Joe speak at her kitchen table, and she thought as she listened: I am dreaming.

She wasn't over the shock of this person, Joe, here at all. Joe — her grandson? And before she was allowed to even think things through, he had launched himself into this. This story of Matt.

Matt. Matthew. It was this boy's father's name. And this boy's father was her son. For so long he hadn't had a name, in her mind. She had kept herself from guessing or from giving him one.

"So then he was in the hospital," the boy continued, looking past her as he spoke, hands crossed on the kitchen table. "They had him on all of these, like, crazy painkillers, I guess? He had morphine and all of that, you know? So Mom and me and my little brother were in there all the time with him and he was all doped up. I don't even think he knew we were there half the time."

"But he's okay?" Renee said. "He's out of the hospital?"

"Yeah," said Joe, turning his eyes to look at her, now that she'd finally said something. His eyes — there was something in his eyes that was just not in Adam's eyes. "He's okay. He sits around all the time at home and I think he's driving my mom crazy at the house, though. He messes around in the garage all day. I think he's depressed. Plus, now he doesn't have a job."

"I'm sorry," she said. "I'm sorry, Joe. I don't understand how you found me. I don't understand what made you come here."

"That was my mom."

"Your mom."

"Yeah. She found you, like, six or seven years ago, I think. I mean, she had some guy find you. I have no idea how he did it. I don't really know any of this. She just paid him, and he went away for a week and he came back and he gave her your name. But I didn't know until just now. She didn't tell any of us that she did it. She just told me about you last week."

"Your father doesn't know who I am then, you're saying? He doesn't know that you're here?"

"No."

"Your mother didn't tell him, still?"

"No."

Renee leaned back in her seat, thinking.

Joe watched her and said, "I know. I mean, I don't know. Don't feel bad if it seems messed up to you. My mom's kind of a weird person."

"Weird?" Renee said. "Weird how?"

"She just — does things. She makes, like, plans. She has all these plans."

"Plans to send you here to talk to me," she said.

"Yeah," he said. "Weird, huh?"

When Renee didn't say anything, Joe put his elbows on the table and scratched at his cheek. "So you wanna know another weird thing?" he asked.

"Okay," said Renee.

"I've read every single one of your books," he said. "Every one. Which is weird because you're, like, the lady on the back of all the books I read when I was a kid, but I'm right here in your kitchen, talking to you." Joe scratched his cheek again. "So that's totally weird."

Joe didn't know exactly what to think when she stood up and asked him if they could take a walk. He didn't care one way or the other, and now she was starting to look not well.

She said, "I just have so many questions, but I can't — I'd like to go out, perhaps? The house feels..." She trailed off.

He said, "It's getting colder again. Do you care?"

"No," she said. "I don't. It's okay. I like the cold."

She had her hand down flat on the table and was looking around as though she'd lost something. The phone started to ring, and she didn't move to answer it.

Joe stayed still in his seat, half expecting her knees to buckle and for her to fall face-first onto the floor right in front of him.

Seeing her so out of sorts made Joe feel more at ease. She looked older than she did in the pictures. Also, in the pictures she had a big smile, and now it was more like a thin, confused moving up and down of the lips. He was glad she hadn't asked him whether he actually had liked any of her books. They'd all been cute. They weren't exactly bad, but just so cute. He had planned a response to the question, though, just in case, because he was not about to walk up to this woman and say, Hi, ma'am, you're my dad's long-lost mom, and also by the way your books totally eat it. If she asked, he was going to tell her that he couldn't remember the actual stories well but he knew that he had liked them because he could remember the thousand times his dad had sat down on his bed and read them to him, so that made it just a good feeling. It was a way to get around the question by saying something true. Joe had a problem in that he never lied.

"I just need my keys," she said, drifting over to the other side of the kitchen. Joe stood up and went to the front door and waited for her there. On the wall he saw a picture of her and what must have been her family, a husband and a son. The husband was bald and had a big goofy smile. The son was taller, with brownish hair. Joe reached into his back pocket and pulled out his gloves. He slid them on, still studying the picture.

Joe's mom was weird. His mom was actually crazy. The whole drive down this morning (Marissa had said, "If you get a speeding ticket, I will kill you, and this won't be such a sweet story after all, will it?"), he had thought about how she'd come home one day with a bag of books, the entire Renee Owen oeuvre, how she'd said an article had said these particular books were good for children, and how she'd then made Matt be the one to go into the boys' room and read to them, even though he was tired. His dad did it, too. Almost every night for a year or two, until they were through with all the books. Matt used to read with funny voices. Maybe they hadn't all been that bad. A couple had been okay if you could get past the cheese.

As for this particular plan, Marissa had come to Joe in the living room just last week and had explained to him how he would be driving down to Chicago to deliver a message to Matt's mother.

He'd been sitting with his feet up on the table, watching TV. It was just the two of them in the house. It was a few months since the fire at Delco. Matt was still at his physical therapy, and Chris was at his guitar lesson.

"What?" he said.

"Your father's mother," she said, standing beside the table, "lives in this suburb by Chicago. The woman is only a hundred miles away." She had printed a map off the computer, along with driving directions. She held them out to him. "Go meet her."

He turned off the TV. He set the remote down in his lap and reached up and took the papers.

"How do you know where Dad's mom lives?"

"Because I know," she said, crossing the room and going back to the kitchen. She called to him from there. "Can you go on Monday?"

Joe stood and went into the kitchen. He looked down at the papers and looked back at her. She was sitting at the kitchen table now. A half-finished crossword puzzle was in front of her. "Why would I go?" he asked. "What am I supposed to say to her?"

"I'll tell you what to say to her," she said. "It's not like it's going to be hard. It's going to be easy. The reason that you have to go is that you have a driver's license, and I can't just disappear all day on Monday because Mr. Grumpy Burn Victim would get all out of sorts and not know what to do with himself."

And now here he was, walking down the street with Ms. Renee Owen, children's author, his father's mother.

She hadn't said anything since they'd left the house. Her jacket was long, cream-colored, all the way down to her ankles. She had a maroon cap and she walked with her hands in her pockets. She walked fast. It looked like she was thinking.

"It's better out here," she said finally. "Thank you. You were right. It is colder. Brr." Since the afternoon it must have dropped twenty degrees. The light outside was getting softer; it would be dark in just a couple of hours. Joe thought of driving back home through the night.

"Joe," she said.

"Yes?"

"Are you my grandson, then?"

"I'm adopted."

"Oh," she said. "I see."

They walked in silence for a minute or two.

He couldn't tell if she was angry. Up ahead he could see the main intersection and the suburb's little downtown area. The bookstore, he remembered, was right there. Once, he thought she would turn off down another side street, but she kept going straight, and soon they were waiting at a stoplight.

"Why did your mother never tell him where I was?"

"Because she wanted him to find you on his own, I think." Marissa had said as much.

"But what made her change her mind?"

"Because I think he's always gone back and forth," Joe said, "and almost tried to find you and then stopped, then almost tried to find you again. For a few years, he was about to — I don't know. I mean, I was little. Mom said, though, that when he was in there, in the hospital? She said that he said things. When he was all drugged up."

"Said things?"

"Yeah."

"Said what?"

Joe looked away, down the street. He was telling her too much.

The car was parked there, across from the bookstore. He'd left it there all day and had been walking around, waiting for her to come home. He hadn't wanted to talk to her there.

"Listen," Joe said. "You know what? I actually think I have to go."

"Oh," she said, surprised. She turned to her left and pointed to an orange-and-white sign. "I was about to offer to buy you a donut."

"That's okay," Joe said.

"You said that so suddenly," Renee said. "Did I somehow — did I say something to offend you?" She smiled at him, shook her head. "Why are you going? You just got here."

"No, no," Joe said. "Not at all, you didn't offend me. I'm just —" He reached into his back pocket and removed the folded envelope. He unfolded it for her, held it out. "I'm actually not supposed to tell you anything else. My mom really wanted me to just tell you, like, basics."

Renee was looking at the envelope.

"She told me to just be the emissary," Joe said.

"Emissary?" She was still looking at the envelope.

"You know," he said. "Greeter."

"What's this?" Renee said.

"From him."

"How, from him?"

"He wrote it on one of those days," Joe said. "When he got into one of those moods and decided he was going to find you. My mom said he actually wrote it the day my little brother was born."

She took the envelope.

"Our phone number's written on the back right there," he said.

Renee turned the envelope over, looked at the number, then turned it back. "And your mother —"

"She stole it out of his glove compartment," Joe said. "Yeah. So yeah, it's not sealed. I mean, she read it. I read it, too, actually. Sorry. I think he just thought he was going to go out and find you and then he just didn't."

"No, no, no," Renee said. "It's okay."

She was still staring down at the envelope.

"So I'm gonna go," Joe said. He took a step back. "So I'll see you, maybe? Or talk to you? Or something?"

She leaned back and looked straight up at the sky. "My God," she said. "Is it snowing? It's supposed to be spring."

Joe looked up, too. He noticed a few flakes coming down.

"It got cold again."

"It did," she said. "You're right."

"Well."

"Are you sure you'll be safe to drive home?" she said.

"I'll be okay," he said. "Snow's okay."

"I get so worried about people driving in the snow," she said.

He stepped away again, just in case she tried to hug him.

"Okay," he said. "It was nice meeting you. Good-bye."

She finally let the hand that held the envelope drop down. She looked at him, nodded, and said, "You have to go."

Joe turned and walked down the sidewalk toward the car.

"Joe?"

He turned.

"It's just that — will he know? When you get home, will you tell him that you were here?"

"I think my mom's telling him," Joe said. "Now. So."

"Oh," she said. "Yes. That makes sense." She raised her eyebrows. "Does that make sense?"

Joe looked down the sidewalk toward the car. He looked back at her. "Do you want me to tell him something for you?" he asked. "I can."

"No," she said, shaking her head. "Oh, no. No. That's okay. No. That's not necessary."

"Are you sure? Because I can."

Renee again shook her head. "I will," she said. "I mean I will do it."

Joe got in the car and started the engine and watched her in the rearview mirror. He thought that maybe she would open it now and read it right here, which would make things easier. He'd thought that she might even read it right in front of him on the sidewalk. But she hadn't. He leaned forward and pulled a copy of the letter from his other pocket, unfolded it, laid it out on the steering wheel, flattened it, and again looked back at her through the mirror. She hadn't moved. She was staring at the Dunkin' Donuts. He waited. She didn't open the envelope. Instead she stuffed it into her coat pocket, turned, and walked back the way they had come. Some bushes blocked his view, and he cut the engine and got out of the car.

He felt bad about copying the letter, as though he'd somehow betrayed his father. But it was important. There had to be a copy of it. Who knew what she would end up doing with hers? For all he knew, she was on her way back to her house to burn it in the fireplace. He took a few slow steps down the sidewalk, and at the corner, he leaned forward just enough to see around the bushes.

There had to be a copy, that's all. She was walking back toward the house.

He waited for just another minute, until she was a speck, a good distance away, before he started after her. Maybe he'd be able to see through a window.

This was his own plan. His mother had hers, and he had his. This had nothing to do with what his mother had told him to do. This was only him. And he didn't really understand what it was that he needed to see or why he needed to see it, exactly. He knew only that it seemed to matter, collecting all the things — the images of people he saw, what they looked like when they said certain words, how they were at certain times and what he guessed they were feeling. He wanted to remember every single thing that happened. Not just here, with her. He did it all the time. His mother couldn't stand it, the way he asked questions, the way he probed, and she would absolutely for sure lose her mind if she could see what he was doing now. But he couldn't help himself. He made a copy of the letter, and he would keep it, and now he was going to watch her read it, if he could, and try to see what she looked like, and if he saw that, he would keep that, too. In this case he had not been able to stop thinking of the moment when she would open it and see his father's writing and read what he said, and for the first time would have an actual thing, there, in her hand, that would show her he had grown into a person.

Joe crossed to the other side of the road, hands in his sweatshirt pockets, and tried to keep pace. He doubted she would look back. He was surprised when she turned on a road they hadn't been on — she wasn't going back to her house.

The snow was picking up a bit. He took a few jogging, hustled steps, and at the corner he again paused and leaned to see. There was the tan speck of her coat. She was still going. He followed her down a long winding street of small homes, keeping the same distance, and he followed her as she made two more turns.

When he made the second turn, he wasn't as careful, though, and he had to jump back behind a hedge. She had stopped. She was across the street, a hundred feet away, in a park. She was sitting on a bench. Joe squatted down a little and was glad that he could see her — he felt certain this was where she'd read it. He watched her sitting with excellent posture, both feet on the ground, both hands on her knees. She looked like a painting, there in the snow. It was coming down at an angle, slowly, but the flakes were big and wet. He reached into his pocket and took the letter out. He held it in his hand, then looked up at her. He waited. If he could read it just as she did, that would be perfect. That would be as close as you could get. He had already read it, but he could do it again, or just skim it as she read it.

She reached into her pocket and took the envelope out.

Joe looked down at his copy, looked back at her. She had it out of the envelope now. She brushed her hair back. Joe looked down and started reading his copy.

July 7, 1997

Dear _____,

If you are getting this letter it means I have finally found
you, or maybe just found your mailing address. My name is
Matthew J. Bishop. I am the son you gave up for adoption
in June 1969. I am sorry to intrude if you aren't able to
know me.

I am writing this letter because my son was born this morning. I don't have your address yet, not today, as I write, but I'm going to find it, I've decided.

On the one hand maybe you don't care about me or where I am or who I am or that I had a son today. If that's so then please disregard this letter. I apologize for taking your time.

If that is not the case, you've probably lived for a long time wondering about things, just as I have. If you're that kind of person then I'm writing to say I'm here, and I'm okay, and it's okay, what you did, I have lived an okay life.

My wife's name is Marissa. Our new boy's name is Chris. He is seven pounds, nine ounces, and he is seven hours old. He has expressed an interest in knowing you in the future.

Sincerely,
Matthew J. Bishop

Joe looked up. He couldn't tell if he had read it faster than she or if she was just not reacting. She was sitting perfectly still on the bench.

The snow kept coming. He felt as though he could crouch here and watch forever and she might never move. The big wet flakes dropped down into his eyelashes, and he blinked them away.

She moved a little. She lowered the hand that held the letter.

Then all at once she tilted some, there on the bench, and her face went down to her other hand and stayed there.

Joe didn't know what to do. He thought the wiser way of

watching would be to stay here, crouched and hidden, but some force compelled him to stand up. You shouldn't always only watch, some voice said. He put his hands in his sweatshirt front pocket. Do more than only watch. He looked around. There was no one anywhere, it seemed. Renee Owen was still hunched over but moving now. Her maroon hat had fallen off and was in the snow at her feet. He watched her reach down and brush it off and look at it, then look at the trees at the other end of the park.

He took a few steps forward, out into the middle of the street, and she turned her head and saw him then, standing there, watching her, and she sat up straight and looked back at him.

He was too far away to see her face clearly, and now there was too much snow. He waited. So did she.

Then he felt the force again, this time at his shoulder and his elbow. Slowly, the boy's hand went up into the air, and he waved.

14

Darren the Human's promise was fulfilled five weeks later when the papers came back from Minnesota with his signature on them. By that time the baby was born. Marissa's labor came in the middle of the night, and she screamed for the last ten minutes in the car on the way to the hospital, saying, "I can't even sit!" Joe stayed back at the house with Glen, and four hours later, another child came into the world.

It was healthy. Matt stood in his scrubs and felt like an idiot as he watched the whole unveiling and watched his sweating wife yell out from the pain, but then the red and wet and pink baby was suddenly there, arrived and human, crying, upside down in the doctor's arms, and not long after that it was in Marissa's arms, and she was smiling and crying at the same time, her face shining and her body spent. She said, "Come on," to Matt, who was still at the other side of the room, and he walked over to his new son and touched him on the forehead as Marissa stroked his face. "You're lucky," Marissa said. "At least this one looks like you."

Matt took a longer time looking at the baby later, when Marissa was asleep. He stared down through the glass. He didn't think it looked like him. It was a pile of flesh. It barely had a face. How could it look like him? Maybe in the eyes. Maybe a little bit. But beyond that he couldn't tell.

"Matt."

Matt turned. There was Glen. Standing beside him was Joe. The two were holding hands.

Glen smiled just a little and said, "Thank God everyone is safe. Is this him here?" He nodded at the glass.

"It is."

Glen came up and looked down through the glass at all the babies, several straight lines of moving, defenseless life. Here they were. And what would happen to them? Matt tried to push his mind to make them each grow, one by one, right before his eyes. He imagined men and women expanding. He looked from one child to the next, wondered which would suffer most. Which would die youngest. Which would cause the most grief for someone else. And he knew that amid all the children, one would love the most, too, and one would sacrifice the most and be the most dignified, and so on. There were no answers to the riddle, but what Matt did see, staring through that glass, was the hidden cradle, invisible, nevertheless trenchant. In it one could place all manner of life and hurt, and still, no matter what, the human could grow with fresh eyes and enter into new realms almost as if by choice. Do anything to it and the human could grow.

"Which one?" Glen asked, and Matt realized Glen had no idea.

"That's him there," Matt said, and pointed, and he stepped back.

Behind him he could see, just barely, that Glen's shoulders shuddered as he looked down.

Matt stepped farther away to let him look at his new grandson, and then he put his hand down on Joe's shoulder and said, "Hey there, little man. Wanna see too?" Joe nodded. Matt squatted and picked him up and brought him forward, and all three of them looked at the sleepy little thing.

"Did you name him?" Glen asked.

"I'm still pushing for Tyrone," Matt said. "I don't think I'm going to get my way."

"No?" Glen asked, smiling. "You never know. Sometimes my daughter will surprise you."

"Yes," Matt said. "Agreed."

In this case, she didn't. Matt didn't really care about what his name ended up being. They named him Chris, after a boy Marissa had known in high school who'd died in a car accident. She said she had remembered him out of the blue. So this new Chris was a healthy, robust young baby, and when they brought him home, they had a whole setup for him, a whole white, sparkling new crib that Matt had found on sale at Target. They had blankets everywhere and toys above the bed, and they had electronic noise monitors. They spared no expense. They turned the little storage room and office into a room for the baby, and they turned the guest bedroom, for the time being, into Joe's room. It was possible that Matt would have to do a little building, as they were running out of space, but for now, and the fall, and the winter, what they had would be fine.

As for the actual cradle, Matt never had a clue. Where it had gone or what had become of it. He figured it had probably been sold to some antique store for fifty dollars. Maybe one day it would end up at someone else's yard sale.

The simple truth was that the cradle was gone. It didn't seem to matter. Not to Glen, not to Matt, not to Marissa. Especially not to Marissa. All that time he'd been away looking, all those things he'd done, all those thoughts he'd had in the meantime, and he'd driven back home after telling her he had it when he did not. He'd found it and lost it. But it was the strangest thing. Matt came home with no cradle at all, with Joe instead, and Marissa never once asked him where it was. In fact, she never brought it up again.

Acknowledgments

Thanks, in no particular order, to Bridget Delaney, Tom and Sarah Grimm, Sara Prohaska, Lee Somerville, Steve Somerville, Mark Rader, Maggie Vandermeer, Oliver Haslegrave, Brettne Bloom, Benjamin Warner, Jenny Jackson, Lucille Collin, and Ben and Sarah Weyenberg. Thanks as well to my beautiful new wife (and shrewdest reader of character psychology), Alexis Jaeger. Special thanks to Ann Buechner, true author of Renee's poem and a wonderful poet herself. A warm hello and thanks to all my friends, mentors, and colleagues from the Cornell writing program, who gave me many years of community and encouragement as a writer. Such things are rare. And finally, thanks to the Virginia Center for the Creative Arts, where most of this book was written. The horses helped.

About the Author

Patrick Somerville grew up in Green Bay, Wisconsin, attended the University of Wisconsin-Madison, and later earned his MFA in creative writing from Cornell University. He is the author of the story collection *Trouble* (Vintage, 2006), and his writing has appeared in *One Story*, *Epoch*, and *The Best American Nonrequired Reading 2007*. He lives with his wife in Chicago and is currently the Simon Blattner Visiting Assistant Professor of Creative Writing at Northwestern University. This is his first novel.